STAY AWAY FROM
LIONS

J. Matthew Smith
and
Patrick Reynolds

N
Buffalo,

Copyright © 2016 J.Matthew Smith and Patrick Reynolds

Printed in the United States of America

Smith, J. Matthew/ Reynolds, Patrick

Stay Away From Lions/Smith and Reynolds- 1st Edition

ISBN: 978-0692622148

1. Stay Away From Lions. 2. Crime Fiction. 3. Buffalo, New York. 4. Noir.
5. Smith and Reynolds

Cover photograph courtesy of Library of Congress, Prints & Photographs Division, Detroit Publishing Company Collection, [reproduction number, e.g., LC-D4-10865]

Inside photographs and back cover photograph © Steve DeMeo

NFB
<<<>>>
No Frills Buffalo/Amelia Press
119 Dorchester Road
Buffalo, New York 14213

For more information visit
nofrillsbuffalo.com

For Dolores 'Lil' Simoncelli Smith
and
in memory of Brian E. Murphy, Buffalo's ultimate
ambassador. See you when I get there.

Stay Away From Lions

Prologue

To the more dignified people north of the Buffalo River it was commonly referred to as "Times Beach." In the Irish neighborhoods that surrounded it on three sides in South Buffalo it was generally called "Seawall Beach" for the cold rock barrier that kept Lake Erie at bay—most of the time.

To those who lived there it was simply "The Beach".

Sure enough, there was a sliver of sand that outlined a strand of the eastern-most edge of Erie in what looked like the shape of an anvil. But this was not Long Island's Hamptons downstate in what may as well have been a whole other world away. It wasn't even the Canadian beaches so close over the border you could canoe there (and many Beachers did to move Canadian alcohol to and fro during Prohibition). In fact, in typical Buffalo Januaries and Februaries, people could walk between the two countries across the ice, although it was not advisable.

No, this wasn't a vacation destination. It was a squatter camp. Rising to the sky just off the beach, Buffalo's hulking grain *elevators rose like fingers and held The Beachers in the palm of their hands and alternately the hollow of their iron fists. There was no escaping their shadow.*

As the nineteenth century reluctantly gave way to the twentieth, The Beach's shantytown was estimated at between one thousand and four thousand people. Overwhelmingly Irish Catholics, they were all but indentured servants to the mills. Most operated as "Scoopers" loading and unloading the elevators with grain. From there, it floated on huge barges east up the Buffalo River or west into the lake for Canada or the Midwest.

The work was brutal. Dusty and scorching in the summer, dusty and frigid in the winter, it was physical, backbreaking work. Many the off-the-boat Beacher asked himself while wiping the dust from his eyes if he was better off here or back in Ireland, famine or no.

South Buffalo had bars. The Beach had bottles. Passing one around the campfire that was the only source of light if not heat, they asked each other in weary brogues if there wasn't a better way. They thought and drank and drank some more before turning in for the night—the five o'clock wakeup moving ever closer. Most had little shacks made up of wood from old shipping crate containers and pieces of corrugated tin scavenged from around the mills. Others had no more than lean-tos—even in Buffalo's unrelenting winters. Still others just curled up on the ground, wrapped around their bottles and halfway to the graves that awaited them.

There was no law but force. The camp was set up in this inhospitable scrap of land because it was just outside of where the tax collectors made their rounds. There were no services of any kind. No quarter was given. None asked for. For all intents and purposes, Beachers were feral. Some arrived so from the old country. Some went native to survive. Or forget.

As their number grew — the big mill corporations' only constraint at the time was labor, so they imported hungry souls from Ireland as quickly as their fastest ships could cross the Atlantic — conditions became markedly worse. The new recruits were angry and disillusioned when they realized they'd been duped, trading in one kind of squalor for another. The haggard veterans who'd been there for years didn't want to hear their tales of woe because they'd become hardened to this place and didn't want to either be reminded of their pitiful plight, or tortured with the sounds and stories of their home.

The new ones didn't know the rules or simply chose not to respect them. Clashes over makeshift benches or slit-trench latrines could turn deadly. Most began with fists. Some escalated to broken bottles or shards of steel fashioned into knives. While they were all in it together, they all looked out for themselves first and foremost.

As stories of Beacher savagery made their way to the regular city folk, the papers seized the opportunity to sensationalize the situation— 'Irish drunks killing one another while living like savages.'

Well-heeled ladies fretted from a great distance about the children—rumored to be multitudinous as litters—and their welfare. The 'lace curtain' Irish one generation or one degree of separation removed from The Beach told their children about the shameful 'shanty Irish' as a cautionary tale of when God and The Church were displaced on the altar by the whiskey bottle and the carnal body.

In the end, it wasn't concern for their well-being or souls that drove a stake through The Beach.

It was profits.

Railroads were replacing ships as the primary means of moving product to market. They were faster and more efficient; moving over land in straighter lines. The New York Rail Road wanted to annex The Beach before the Pennsylvania Railroad got there first. With the mill owners' permission and full support, they began forcibly evicting Beachers in order to lay tracks. They'd lay it one day only to find it torn up the next. Guards were brought in to watch the worksite overnight. Clashes with Beachers were common, but usually not fatal. Many of the police were Irish too. They looked down their noses at the squatters, hard-

ened criminals nearly all, but they were still Irish. There was still that bond. Most of the harassers huffed and puffed, but when the watchmen's black jacks came out, they slunk away.

On September 2, 1901 workers were busily laying track at a fevered pace. Interestingly, these were not Irish immigrants. They weren't immigrants at all. The railroad was the next rung up the labor ladder. The pay wasn't great, but it wasn't bad. There was a certain amount of civility and rationality to it that did not exist for scoopers. Ten-hour shifts, five days a week, over-time when the job required, were all standard fare.

Around three o'clock a woman was walking along the tracks without saying a word. She wore a loose garment with a black shawl covering her shoulders and falling half-way down her back. She was barefoot.

A big German was dropping the railroad tie into place nearest to her. She stopped beside him.

"What does 'eminent domain' mean?"

The laborer turned and looked, not saying anything. In retrospect, he may not have known.

His partner on the other end of the tie spoke up. He was Irish, but his brogue was long gone. He'd been in America for some time and had a bed every night he was in the New World.

"It's a fancy way of sayin' 'what's mine is mine.' Nobody owns it so I claim it. What are you askin' for?" he said somewhat

kindly.

"I've heard people goin' on about it but wasn't sure they got it right."

The big German wiped his brow and, turning his back to her, pulled his gloves back on.

She went on.

"So why then isn't this shithole not fit for man or beast ours by 'eminent domain'? There was fish and vermin here before us. Nothing more."

The German didn't even turn around. It wasn't that he was unsympathetic to her plight. He didn't even let it enter his mind. He had a job to do. It was above his pay grade to even consider such things. He was a workhorse with blinders, just pulling the plow.

His partner responded, less sympathetic this time.

"I guess the Mills' 'eminence' is greater than yours at the end of the day. It's all their domain."

He too pulled on his gloves and bent over to grab the next tie.

She pulled an eighteen-inch hand axe out from under her shawl. With every bit of the fury demonstrated by the Seneca warriors who hunted in that same spot two-hundred years before, she brought it down into the right shoulder-blade of the big German. It buried to the hilt.

"Then fuck yiz all."

++++++++

Ten of them dragged the tarp straight into the middle of the camp. Beachers came out from all over with lanterns and even crude torches. None said a word. There were twenty cops on horseback—five in front and back, five left and right. They said nothing but reared the horses up in the direction of anyone who came too near.

The workers dropped the bundle in the middle of the camp. They got to one side and unfurled it like they were throwing out a picnic blanket.

The woman's body laid face up. Her own hatchet was stuck in her forehead dead between the eyes.

The Irishman from the tracks looked at as many faces as he could make out in the flickering light.

"Fuck yiz all."

++++++++

The following day the dead woman's baby was left on the stairs of the Catholic Church that bordered the camp to the south in what is present day Tift Farm.

It was a girl.

CHAPTER ONE

Look, I never proclaimed to be some sort of perfect goddamn Catholic. I'd like to think God gives us credit for trying. So, if I go to confession and I lie about my sins, well, in my mind, it's still a helluva lot better than not going at all. There's a certain sanctity in going through the motions. The same applies to church. I'm not goddamn stupid. I know when I'm at Mass that I shouldn't be checking out women. But I mean, I'm a man. It's a natural impulse for me to want to hop on a nice piece of tail, and if I'm being totally honest here, church is one of the best places to scope talent. Always has been — especially Easter Mass when all the women are dressed to the nines. So, yeah, I know that's wrong, but it's not like I spend the entire Mass doing it. And, like I say, at least I'm there, which is a hell of a lot more than I can say for most Catholics. Besides, the way I see it, the Church is lucky I'm even willing to attend Mass considering all the gross shit its priests have been doing to altar boys over these past few decades or longer.

My friends growing up were altar boys and they always

had the best scams. They told me that when the church was empty, they would take the long matches that parishioners used to light prayer candles, stick them in the donation slots, and clear out all the money. Genius. I couldn't pass up the opportunity. So, when Mass wasn't being held, I'd ride my bike to church with my buddies and swipe money from the prayer candles and then blow it all on cigarettes and 'Asteroids' at the video arcade down the street. Years later, one of my buddies and I even lifted a collection plate, which we pissed away on a few bottles of Mad Dog 20/20. Youthful indiscretions.

When I got older, I felt tremendous guilt over that and worried about going to Hell. But then once all the sex stuff started coming out about the priests, I figured my sins paled in comparison to what was actually going on inside the Church itself. So, figuring God had much larger fish to fry, I took a mulligan on the whole prayer-candle thing and put a fifty dollar bill in the collection basket one Sunday. There — it was now a wash. And, yeah, I swiped that fifty from someone's wallet at a bar; but still, I paid my debt back to the Church. Circle of life. Nobody ever really owns money anyway. We're all just holding it until somebody takes it away from us one way or the other.

***

That was just about two years ago. A hundred Sundays have passed—give or take. After buying my indulgence from the Church in the grand tradition of Kennedys and killers before me, 'a subtle distinction' my old man used to say to torment my mom, I found myself less distracted at church. A big issue was off the table and off my mind. With that, my ears and eyes were more open. Instead of being preoccupied with myself and all the women I wanted to jump, I noticed things. I wasn't reformed to the point of paying actual attention to the real message of the actual Mass. This wasn't a miracle and I sure as shit ain't ever been no altar boy. But I was paying attention. Who dragged their kids? Who was dragged by their husband or wife? Who sang? Who mouthed the words? Who used the old prayers? Who used the Vatican Two, gender-neutral, politically correct, bullshit ones? Who even knew this new fucking pseudo-Protestant conversational shit? It was a lot to take in.

But take it in I did.

Time passed more quickly. The hour felt half that. If there was an early football game, the exactly thirty-five minutes felt like fifteen. Everyone's attention span in Buffalo is short on the Sunday morning before a Bills game — even the clergy's. God's a betting man. And knowing what he knows about the Bills, he's usually betting on the visitor.

One Fall Sunday the church was jammed. Just packed.

I figured some obscure Holy Day of Observation only the aged knew or cared about. I was there because I was playing the game. They came because they were obliged. I'm not sure which is worse. But at this particular Mass we were elbow-to-elbow. Some even stood in the back, younger men, mainly, who despite their general lack of common sense at least had the courtesy to give up their seats to the old and infirmed making up the over-whelming majority of the faithful.

Fucking patsies.

***

I've got a bad knee. See, last time I was in county, I tore my meniscus during a fight with my cellie after finding out he'd stolen a cell phone I'd hidden inside my bunk frame. I was whipping his ass pretty good, but he was a lard-ass, outweighing me by probably a good seventy pounds or so. Despite the tension in lock up, I've always managed to go along and get along. You watch your back, but as long as you play by jailhouse rules, don't go looking for trouble, and aren't in there for anything disgusting like diddling a kid, you'll survive.

Anyway, as I was pounding away on this fat son-of-a-bitch, he fell forward on top of me. We crashed to the ground with my leg stuck behind me. I could feel my ligament snap. I'll admit it: the guards — who responded after hearing the com-motion caused by our fall — probably saved my ass. There was no way I was going to get that obese motherfucker off of me, especially with the pain shooting through my leg. This is why, incidentally, when I'm inside I don't give staff any trouble. I will never understand these maniacs who throw their shit and piss on guards and then expect them to rescue their ass when they're in trouble. If someone tossed their shit at me one day and then found themselves getting their ass kicked and in need of help the next, I can assure you I'd turn my fucking head and walk away. There is a law to the jungle.

Anyway, as I was saying, because of my bad leg, I can't kneel when I'm in church. So, when the rest of the parishioners were on their knees, I remained standing, which provided me a bird's eye view of the congregation. And that's when I spotted her, third in from the center aisle in a pew in the middle of the church. It was the first time since walking out of county five months ago that I had seen her, and if you add in the nine months I spent inside — (three months less than the twelve to which I was sentenced thanks to overcrowding) — it had been more than a year.

She looked beautiful. I mean she always looked beautiful. But there was just something about the way she looked at that moment in particular, kneeling there all calm and at peace, that made her look especially gorgeous. Maybe it had something to do with the light streaking through the stained glass onto her chestnut hair. Or, maybe it was because she didn't look tired anymore. I realize being with me is no walk in the park. I exhausted her, and when I was sentenced to a year for assault — (originally a felony charge before being lowered to misdemeanor third-degree) — she made it clear that she had nothing left. And she meant it. Not only did she never visit me while I was inside, she never called and she never wrote. She cut all ties.

"I can't do it anymore," she said calmly. "I can't do it. I'm done."

It was the calmness. That's how I knew she wasn't fucking around this time. Women are emotional creatures. Most of the time, their reactions are influenced by their feelings. They act primarily with passion and usually with little thought. It's when they're calm and measured that they mean business. She wasn't reacting based on her feelings because she was no longer feeling anything. And I can't say I blame her.

* * *

When Mass ended, I hung around the back. Everyone else had cleared out, the altar boys running down the aisle to meet their parents outside. Game day. They understood the urgency. After all, there are three recognized religions in Buffalo: Catholicism, bowling and the Buffalo Bills. And Ralph Wilson Stadium is the Vatican.

Father Frank came out in his civvies—black on black,

collar, no stole and snuffed the candles. He must have been in his mid-sixties, but he still had the crew cut and Popeye forearms harkening back to his days as a service chaplain. He was a soldier for God. We weren't at war (God and us), but Father Frank was ready if and when the celestial gloves dropped. He was a tough bastard.

"Father?"

"I cannot bless your bets, your bookmakers, or bring locusts upon your gambling enemies, Tommy. God only knows how you'll cover an eleven-point spread with that defense."

"And He ain't telling."

"So it seems."

"Got time for a confession?"

"Eight minutes by my watch."

"Then let's get started. I've got lots to get off my chest."

"Haven't we all."

"Not like this."

He moved into the confessional box solemnly. The door clicked shut, echoing throughout the empty church, bouncing off the arches and pillars.

I rubbed my temples and followed. Eight minutes was not enough time. Hell, in my case, neither was eight days.

* * *

There comes a time in every guy's life when he needs to,

as my old man used to say, "either shit or wind his watch." For me, that time was now. Next time I fucked up, I wasn't going back to county. My next stop was the state pen for some hard time.

No question: I was a cat on his last life.

I'm a smart guy. I know the consequences of my actions and always have. Why I've always insisted on taking the risk, I can't exactly say. It was never about the thrill like it is for some guys. I don't need the adrenalin rush. I suppose, instead, it's always been about earning a fast buck. The straight life has never appealed to me. Trudging along from day-to-day at some bullshit job, saving my pennies in the hopes that someday I have enough to buy a pair of new shoes, just seems like a hopeless road to nowhere.

And it ain't like the old days around here, either. Bethlehem Steel is gone. So is Republican Steel. And since America no longer makes anything anymore, Buffalo's unskilled workforce is shit outta luck. If you do happen to hold down a job in this city, which is now one of the nation's poorest, you're barely scraping by. And the unions that ran things forever? All gone. 'I got your organized labor right here' said the starched, corporate overlords. They picked up their marbles—no—they picked up *our* marbles and went home to their beaches, New York City penthouses and fake tits. We got stuck with the tab, snow, and the fucking Bills. Boobs, yeah, but no fake tits.

Shit, I don't know one single fucking guy living straight who's walking around with a fat wad of cash in his pocket. But when I was on the street, I had a fresh stack everyday. And yeah, sometimes I'd feel a bad about how I earned that money, but not for long. In my mind, it was business. Look, either you're gonna fuck me or I'm gonna fuck you. That's how it works. The business world is a nasty place: whether it's the straight world or my world. I'd rather be the fucker than the fucked, and every guy I knew living straight was being fucked — and not in a good way. No fake tits.

But now, I've got no option. I either go straight and try not to get fucked. Or I go back to the street and hope I don't get busted, because if I do, I wind up in prison where I'll spend each and every day, literally, trying not to get fucked.

* * *

The screen slid open.

"Bless me Father for I have sinned. It's been three weeks since my last confession."

"1 Peter 5:8 - Be sober, be vigilant; because your adversary the devil, as a roaring lion, walketh about, seeking whom he may devour."

"Father, I don't have anything specific. I'm just no good." My ears began to ring a little. My eyes were wet and pupils dilated in the confessional dark. I continued, "My whole life I've done stuff. Wrong stuff. Bad stuff. Not really, really bad, but not right either. And I knew it was wrong. But I just wanted to do the wrong thing more than the right one. The path of least resistance, you know?"

"Why do you think that is? What compels you to choose that which you know to be wrong?"

It felt like my throat was closing.

"Down deep I just didn't care. Not enough anyway."

"Your lying before me and before The Father offends us both."

"Not tracking. I am confessing. I am telling the truth. What more do you want me to say? I'm a bum. I'm no good. I'm a sinner. What do you want from me?"

"I have a confession for you, too," said the priest. "I know about the collection plate. I know you pinched it."

"How?"

"Either Divine wisdom or someone named names in this very confessional."

"I'm surrounded by rats. No wonder I'm such a fuck up."

"Ahem." His nose was clearly right up against the screen now.

"I'm sorry, Father. Forgive me."

"God loves a sinner. Even a foul-mouthed one. And Tommy, I know something else, too. I know you put it back. Repeat that pattern."

He switched from Archangel to regular guy. "Kickoff time. Say five Our Fathers, three Hail Marys and two Glory Bes. Good luck."

"Amen."

"And, Tommy…"

"Yes, Father?"

"Stay away from lions."

CHAPTER TWO

I had five hundred riding on New England. They were minus-6 at Buffalo. Had they been playing at home, the spread would have been larger. But the Pats often suck when they play here. Last year, they had to come from behind to win on a last-minute field goal. And three years ago, Brady tossed four interceptions here in a 3-point loss. Buffalo has a pretty good defense, but their offense isn't anything to write home about — although that never seems to stop the loyalists in this fucking city from believing a Super Bowl championship is right around the corner, my goddamn mother included.

She's an interesting piece of work, that one. Swears like a sailor, smokes like a chimney, drinks like a fish, and made of wire. She's all piss and vinegar except when it comes to the Church, the Kennedys, and the Bills. That's her Holy Trinity. You fuck with them; you'll get a boot in your ass and a thumb in your eye. Love her, but she's scary as fuck.

As for the Bills, well, what this fucking team needs is a quarterback. That hasn't changed since Jim Kelly retired after the 1996 season. I remember watching Kelly's final game, thinking to myself: 'Well, it's all gonna be downhill from here on out.' Rarely am I that right. But I nailed it that time. Since then, Buffalo has seen a non-stop parade of shitty quarterbacks: Todd Collins, Rob Johnson, Trent Edwards, J.P. Losman — the list is endless. Yeah, we had Doug Flutie. Fucking guy was amazing. Yet, despite being 21-9 as a starter for the Bills, the team saw no future in him because he was nearly 40 years old — never mind the fact that all he did was win. Fucking dumbasses.

There's a weird vibe in Buffalo on game day. With the exception of the area around Ralph Wilson Stadium, there's an eerie silence that creeps into the rest of the city. The roads and highways are virtually empty. Save for its bars, Buffalo on a Sunday afternoon is like a ghost town. The calm before the storm. You can almost taste the anticipation leading up to kickoff. It begins on Thursday evenings, when the parking lot at Ralph Wilson stadium begins to fill with tailgaters setting up their campers and RVs and the fanatics in their rented U-hauls with enough kegs to last them through the weekend. Walk into any bank on Friday, and you're likely to be greeted by a teller with red, white and blue war paint on their face. At Sunday Mass, half the congregation shows up in Bills jerseys — some accented by chicken-wing sauce stains.

Even priests.

When I was about twelve, or fifteen maybe, I came home Sunday morning from delivering papers and Father Frank was there. He was in jeans and a grey Bills hoodie. His hair was all over the place. I remember thinking it was weird but the Sunday paper was a bitch with all the fucking inserts so I was too whipped to give it too much thought.

"Father is taking you to the game today," my mother said, herself a vision in a terrycloth housecoat and slippers.

There was a pause before Fr. Frank chimed in. "Yes. Are you ready? We'll stop for breakfast on the way. It'll be fun."

And so we did.

You've heard of the 'Tin Ticket' cops speak of where they flash the badge to get into concerts, sporting events, and so on? Fr. Frank flashed the collar—even when he wasn't wearing one. On this particular day we circled the whole stadium, Fr. Frank craning his neck at every gate until he finally spotted Vinnie Camilo from the parish. Vinnie was a cop who worked security on the side to make a few bucks—and see a few games for free. He was in the quiet Italian mold. He didn't say much, which made him kind of scary. But he didn't harass or bother anyone either, which sort of negated that.

"Vinnie!" Father yelled.

Vinnie waved us over.

"And a lovely day it is. Peace be with you."

"Same to you, Father. Who's this?"

"This is Tommy. Mrs. Patton's son."

They exchanged a bit of a look I noticed.

"Ahh. Sorry to hear about your old man, son. Good guy."

And with that, we were in.

* * *

I decided to watch the game at Murphy's on Ohio Street down in the old First Ward — an area of the city predominantly made up of working-class, Irish families living in the shadows of Buffalo's historic grain elevators — grain elevators that rise to nowhere and have fallen so low. The Ward is from where my family hails. My grandfather worked thirty years as a grain scooper, and my grandmother retired from the General Mills plant, which at night coats the city in the aroma of freshly made Cheerios — a delicious and welcome relief from Buffalo's day-time stench of despair.

I grabbed a seat at the end of the bar, directly in front of the television — the gin-mill equivalent of sitting on the 50-yard-line.

"Shot and a beer, hon," I said to Bridgette who was tending bar.

"Long time no see, Tommy. Where ya been?"

"Whaddy'a mean? It's the first game of the season."

"You know what I mean. You been outta county for a

while now," Bridgette said. "Katie told me you got out."

"She knew?"

"Yeah, she knew. She keeps tabs. So where ya been?"

"Just keeping low. Trying to stay outta trouble."

"Finally."

"Yeah, well... So how's Katie? She ok?"

"She's fine. She's happy."

"I saw her in church today. Holy Family."

"She talk to you?"

"She didn't see me."

"You know she worries about you, Tommy."

"She does, huh?"

"She doesn't want to see you. But she worries. You being good?"

"I told you I was."

"That doesn't mean you're telling the truth. So, you got money on the game today?"

I didn't answer right away. She wanted to hear me say 'no,' but she knew the answer was 'yes.' Old habits, ya know? I'm a good crook but a shitty liar. Always have been.

"Look, I gotta get some money. Gotta get on my feet. I just need to get a little nest under me to, you know, get myself established. I swear I'm going straight. Don't tell Katie, ok?"

"Tommy, I ain't gotta tell Katie anything. I know, and

she knows, you won't ever change," Bridgette said shaking her head. "I won't say anything. But you gotta get your shit together. Good luck. Though I should kick your ass outta here because I know you didn't take the Bills. How fucking dare you put your money on that pretty boy, Brady. It's all about lining your pocket. Like I said, you won't ever change."

* * *

Cliché though it may be, football is a great metaphor for life. You line up across from a guy. Who wants it more? Who's stronger? Who'll put it on the line? Whose cock's like a nine-pound hammer? Who's got a little finishing nail?

It's also about the pack. Looking out for your brother. You fuck with him—you fuck with me. And you fuck with me; there'll be hell to pay. Same as on the street.

That's why in the Rust Belt, football reigns supreme. Tough towns like Pittsburgh, Cleveland, Milwaukee, Detroit, Chicago, and, of course, Buffalo. They like to butt heads at the gin mills and then watch men butt heads on the field. That's religion. That's truth.

Now, though, nobody butts heads. They just blow them off. When did that start? When were dustups no longer settled with fists, a handshake, and a few beers? Funny. Nobody needs a gun more than me, but I fucking hate them. A brawl lasts a few minutes. But you squeeze that trigger and that's forever. My old man used to tell me all the time, "Two seconds of a bad decision can change the rest of your natural life." I can attest, too. The jails are filled with a lot of people wishing they had those two seconds back.

Now this particular game, Bills vs. Pats, offered a bit of a twist on the football-street-life analogy. The Pats were roughly the same size as the Bills. They both probably benched the same, ran as fast... right on down the line.

But what was different was their intellect. The Pats were so much smarter. They had street sense the Bills have never had. I imagine Brady, their poster-boy, cleft-chinned, cock-sucking quarterback, yelling across the line, "Hey (insert defender here), your Ma's a little loose with her cunt, ain't she?" Our guy jumps off-sides, trying to tear his fucking head off, as Brady laughs his way another five yards up the field on their inevitable march to pay dirt.

I hate those faggots. But a little part of me deep down admires them. Brawn without brains can't win. Just enough brains with plenty of brawn will get a ring on your finger. Or four.

* * *

Brawn without brains — kinda explains the difference, too, between the cities that the Bills and the Pats call home. I always thought of Buffalo as a sort-of Boston without the glitz.

Both cities have their Irish working-class roots. Both towns are tough. Their people have a similar no-nonsense attitude about them. But what separates these cities are the brains. In military terms, Buffalo is a grunt. Boston is an officer. Buffalo's pud is in the mud. Boston's penis is golden. Buffalo has a handful of colleges, including the University of Buffalo. Boston has a million colleges, including Harvard, Northeastern and MIT. Buffalo's economy is perpetually struggling. Boston's economy is strong. Buffalo has Millard Fillmore. Boston has JFK. Hands down, I would take Buffalo in a street fight. But I would take Boston in a war. Boston sees the big picture down the line, around the bend. We only see to the end of our fist and the bottom of our beer mug.

In football, a single quarter is a street fight. But, the game in its entirety is a war. Muscle is important, but if you don't use it strategically and wisely, it will only get you so far. And when it comes to strategy and wisdom, there are few who use both better than fucking Brady and Belichick. That's why I bet against the Bills. Yes, it is all about lining my pocket. Absolutely.

Still, I understand Bridgette's disgust. In this city, an act such as mine is high treason. It's the kind of act that in a tough Buffalo bar could lead to a brawl and end with a bullet. So, while watching the game, I try to keep my emotions to myself. No one needs to know who my money's on — especially when such information could be hazardous to my health. These fucking people might live and die by how the Bills do on Sunday, but I'm sure as shit not willing to take a bullet for these goddamn clowns. Yeah, my heart is with them — always will be. But the Bills have been responsible for far too many emotional blows to the gut of this city. Four straight Super Bowl losses, anybody? The Music City Miracle? Fifteen straight years without a playoff appearance? The list is endless. I'm sure as shit not going to let them screw me financially, too.

* * *

Between plays, between halves, I'm thinking back to my confession. Not so much on who ratted me out or why. I'd like to think they're concerned for my soul, but they're probably trying to scrape the shit off the bottom of theirs.

No, I was thinking more about the verse— the "lion." It was interesting. It touched a nerve. Since I'd been out of the can, I had a strong feeling like someone was watching me. Stalking me almost, like a lion hunting its prey. Sometimes I even thought I saw things out of the corner of my eye. Just a bit of shoulder up ahead at the corner. But when I'd get there there'd be nothing. I'd walk on and turn around quick, once more for good measure. I didn't actually see anything, just the vapor trail of something that left in a hurry. I did some acid as a kid. Maybe it was that.

But I don't think so.

When I was a kid there were rare occasions when I would pray. Usually those occasions immediately followed a fuck-up and went something like, "If You keep me from getting my ass handed to me, or thrown in the joint, or being shot… I'll never do this shit again." Sometimes I got a response back, but it was more like a feeling than words. This was the visual equivalent of that. There was someone else there, but maybe that was just my imagination. Basically, I've narrowed it down to God, a hit man, a plain clothes or an artifact of a mind going too fast for too long.

Wouldn't it be funny if it were all of those?

Then it hit me just as the second half was about to begin.

"No fucking way, " I said and laughed.

"You're a fucking beauty," Bridgette said coldly. "Fucking coked up or whatever, muttering to yourself like a fucking loon."

"You know I don't mess with that shit, so it must be the latter. I'm a fucking loon."

But what if it was an angel?

* * *

So it comes to this: I've either lost my mind or I'm paranoid. Someone is either watching out for me, or lying in wait to do me harm. There's either a devil or angel on my shoulder.

Or maybe this is God himself testing me a final time. Either I go straight once and for all, or I fuck up one last time and end up doing hard time.

To be honest, it'd be no surprise if there were a hit man following me. Completely plausible. There are an untold number of people out here who have good reason to want to hurt me. There are people I stole from; people I beat up; people I cheated and people I let down. It's a byproduct of the life I've chosen to live up until now. I'm not seeking pity. If there is, indeed, someone out there who's going to hurt me, it's a fate I brought upon myself. I am willing to lie in the bed I have made for myself.

Having a guardian angel? Now that's fucked up. Delusional really. But if being Catholic is about having faith, then it stands to reason there's people like Father Frank who still have faith in me. Maybe that's crazy. But faith isn't about certainty; it's about trust and hope. I ain't stupid. I know I give just about everyone plenty of reasons not to trust me. But maybe someone like Father Frank sees something in me — whatever it is — that inspires hope. Maybe there's someone connected to the Church following me — laying in wait to step in right before I fuck up.

Either way, what I do know is this: if the fucking Pats don't cover the spread, I'm fucked. I lose this half-a-grand, and it's desperation time. And when things get desperate, the devil on my shoulder always kicks the angel's ass right off.

* * *

The Bills have this sewn up. They'll lose, of course, but they'll lose by four. They'll cover. Bad enough to lose every single close one. Good enough to screw me royally with the book. Lose-lose.

There's only one thing the Bills can do to either save me or give me partial redemption. One minute left. They're getting the ball on a punt. If they put a march together and go down and score, I'll take some solace in knowing we beat those fuckers for what feels like the first time in a thousand years. At least there's that. The bar will erupt. There'll be free drinks. I'll surely get laid.

The other option is they fuck it up and actually get scored on, thereby losing the game *and* not covering.

Yup. They go with option number two, of course. Muffed fucking punt. It hits off a blocker's ass — he never sees it — and the Pats cover inside the Bills twenty. They take a knee on three consecutive plays, but there's too much time on the clock with the Bills using their final timeouts.

They have no choice but to kick a field goal, go up by seven and make me a winner.

The bar goes silent. An old drunk yells something like "Fucking cunts!" in a thick Irish brogue. He was born and raised in the First Ward but for some mysterious reason speaks in an accent when he's drunk. My brother used to joke that the guy was kicked in the head by a leprechaun.

There's a bit of a "same old Bills" murmur, but mostly people are just dejected. In Buffalo, we don't expect to win, but we're constantly amazed at the ways by which we lose. This is yet another in a long list. We could fuck up fake tits.

"I suppose you covered," Bridgette says.

"Same old Bills," I say, noncommittal.

"Seventeen-Fifty."

"Put it on my tab."

"You ain't got a fucking tab."

"Then put it on his tab, " I say, nodding to the guy at the end of the bar.

"I don't know who he is and bet you don't either. Dressed too nice to be from around here. And too nice for a cop."

"Maybe he's undercover."

"There's bigger fish to fry in this town than you nickel and dimers throwing a couple hundred bucks around like you're Al Capone."

"Come with anybody?"

"Nope. Said he'd hold a seat for a bit but nobody came."

"Stood up. The nerve."

"Ordered two beers. Drank them both. Said one was for

him."

"This sounds like the joke about the Irish twins."

"His brother quit drinking. Still a favorite. No, he said the other was for Kingdom Come. Takes all kinds, I guess."

She continued, "Was chatting up with Fr. Frank before you showed. Might have been the other way around actually, now that I think of it."

"Confession?"

"Just a matter of for which sin."

I couldn't help but laugh. Only slightly less common that bargaining with God to never drink again after a particularly violent hangover was telling a bartender you'll never do the sins again that the devil of drink made you do.

* * *

I'd like to hang around and celebrate my financial upswing, but something isn't sitting right. I reach into my front pocket and pull out a ten, which is all I have, and lay it on the bar. Bridgette gives me a look and I flash her a wave.

"I'll be back to settle the rest later," I say as I discreetly shoot a look at the well-dressed stranger at the other end of the bar.

Bridgette says something to me, but I already have my back turned and can't make out what's she's saying. But if I were to place a bet, I'd bet that she wasn't wishing me well and, without a doubt, in doing so, I'd be up even more than the five-hundred clams I won from betting on the game. As I head toward the exit I glance up at the round mirror hanging kitty-corner above the door to see whether I'm being followed.

The stranger stays on his stool. But, and maybe this is just my paranoia speaking, he seems to be watching me too.

I walk out of Murphy's all calm and collected, but as soon as my stride takes me past the front windows, I pick up the pace dramatically and hook a right onto Michigan Avenue. As I walk, I'm playing over and over in my head who might be out to get me and why. The list is long. A little too long, actually. Despite my regular attendance at Mass, I haven't always exhibited the traits of a choir boy. And despite my faith, the guy in the bar, at least judging by his appearance, doesn't exactly look like my fucking guardian angel.

I look over my shoulder but I don't see anyone following. Still, I kick it up a gear and turn right onto South Park. I scurry my way down another block-and-a-half and hide behind a metals shop, which, given that it's a Sunday, is closed for the day. I keep my eyes mostly fixed out front on South Park, but I also pay close attention to my backside just to make sure I'm not surprised from behind like one of Tony Soprano's sorry-ass victims. I pull out my Camels and smoke my last cigarette as I wait — not exactly the wisest decision on my part, I realize, since if a predator is on my trail the smell of cigarette smoke will give me away. At this point, though, I don't give a shit. My nerves are frayed. If I had ten cigarettes left, I'd smoke them all at once.

I reach into my inside-coat pocket and feel around for my blade. Again, not exactly smart on my part to have a weapon on me with my rap sheet, but walking around these streets empty handed is probably even dumber.

After some fifteen minutes, there's still no sign of the well-dressed man. So, I stand up and decide to emerge from hiding. But as I do, I hear the slow approach of a vehicle coming my way down South Park. It's a Cadillac STS. Let me be clear, no one in this neighborhood — a mix of mostly abandoned warehouses and clap-board dwellings home to Buffalo's working poor — owns a Cadillac STS. So, if you see one tooling around these streets, it's either stolen or being driven by someone not from the Ward. And sure as shit, sitting behind the wheel is the man from Murphy's, looking side-to-side out his windows as he inches slowly along South Park.

* * *

"Need a lift?"

"Nah. I don't live too far from here. Fresh air'll do me good."

"Smells like Cheerios to me. Cheerios and stale beer."

"That was the name of my band in high school."

"Cheerios and Stale Beer. One night only."

"So you're that guy who came. I'd wondered all these years."

"I guess we've both changed a bit since then. Then again, maybe we haven't."

"I'm older. Balder. Other than that, exactly the same," I said.

"Good for you. I'm not the same guy. When you're young, you're stupid. You think only about yourself. Always in the short term. Never what's around the corner. You never know what's gonna be around the corner. Or who. With experience, you learn to think bigger picture."

"I guess I'm still seventeen, then. I can't even see your face in there. It's past the edge of my nose."

"Too bad. Well, at least on one hand it is. When you see pieces of the bigger picture, the little things start to make more sense. They're no longer pieces of the picture, but rather pieces of the puzzle. On the other hand, ignorance is bliss. It was great not knowing or not caring even if you did know. You know?"

"It's a sad day when you realize you can't plead ig-norance any more," I said. "Like Eve after the apple. There's shame."

"Maybe you were tricked like she was."

"Wouldn't stand up under cross-examination, I'm

afraid."

"Thought I'd give you an out."

"I appreciate that. So what's next? We're having a nice chat and I don't mean to rush. It's just not every day a complete stranger in a luxury sedan stops to chat me up like this. Especially a stranger such as yourself if you know what I'm saying."

"I understand. You've got a debt to pay, so I'll let you go. I know you were on your way to get your money, so please, don't let me stand in your way. We all want this to end well," he said somewhat ominously.

"Debt?"

"The Lord giveth. The Lord taketh away. Mine is not to judge, just to ensure collections are made. Next week I'm all in on the Lions. You take care, ok?"

He rolled up the windows, banged a U-turn and that was that.

As I watched his Cadillac travel further away, I knew it would return sooner rather than later. I was now in a world of shit, and there was no guardian angel around to protect me.

CHAPTER THREE

So, as you might imagine, the news I had a debt to pay left me a bit unsettled. How the fuck is this possible? I admit I may disappear from time-to-time when I owe someone some cash, hoping the debt will be forgotten. But one-hundred-percent of the time, I'm acutely aware of said debt since I'm typically spending every waking minute looking over my shoulder. And sure, I'll admit too that I'm quite fortunate such a congenial goon was sent after me to provide a gentle reminder — even though this was complete fucking news to me. After all, given his occupation, he could have just as easily decided to deliver his message with a baseball bat... (which no doubt he had in his trunk.) The guy looked like someone you'd have batting cleanup.

The next morning, I lay in bed going over in my head the bets I had placed before my last stint in county. Looking back, I guess it was divine intervention that had kept me from betting on the Super Bowl. I was awaiting sentencing and fortunately had enough sense not to aggravate my situation. Had I lost and wound up owing thousands on the Super Bowl, I certainly would have paid with a broken leg behind bars. The people I usually do business with aren't the types who are willing to forgive a debt due to incarceration. In fact, the wait only tends to piss them off more. When you owe money while in the can, you can bet there's an independent contractor on the inside who's been hired to ensure that in lieu of actual cash, you pay with busted limbs. One way or another, you always pay.

I decided to head down to Bailey's Tap House on Seneca Street, a dark old Irish dive where wearing matching socks is considered pretense. There in the glow of the Fighting Irish sign was Petey, sitting with a cup of coffee and doing his books. He didn't look up but he knew I was there.

"Well, well, if it isn't Thomas James Patton, the Ward's wayward son," Petey said, still staring at his numbers. "If I were a betting man," he went on, now removing his glasses and looking up at me, "and you know that I'm not – I only do business with them – I would never have put money down on you showing your face in these parts again."

"Yeah, well, that's what I'm here to talk to you about," I said, taking a seat. "Look Petey, you know I was away for awhile. If something fell through the cracks in between, I'm sorry. Really. But look, I'm being totally honest. I don't remember any debt. I swear on the soul of my mother and all that is holy. Honest."

"Tommy, my friend. You're a smart kid. You always were. But you've always been a little careless, too. Your balls have always been a little bit bigger than your brain. The good news? You don't owe me anything. We're square…"

"Oh shit, Petey, thank God! Really. This is a fucking weight off my chest, brother. I don't know how to thank you. You have no idea how fucking…"

"Hold on, hold on," Petey interrupted. "The good news is you don't owe me. The bad news is — and this is really fucking bad news, Tommy — you owe Carlo Della Pina. The word's out, kid. And I gotta tell you, if they come to me and ask whether I've seen you, I'm not gonna lie. I have no desire to be tossed in the trunk of my car with my severed penis shoved down my throat. My advice: do what you need to do and get Carlo his money. And Tommy…"

"Yeah?"

"Get it fast."

I wanted to throw up. I could hear Petey talking, but I was so overcome with fear and anxiety I could barely make out what he was saying. I was sweating. Shaking. The room was spinning.

"Oh my fucking God," I whispered. I looked up at Petey. "How much do I owe?"

"Ten grand."

Ten grand. It might as well be a million dollars. How the fuck was I going to come up with ten grand in one week? When you do business with Carlo, you don't forget. But somehow, I did. How the hell did that happen? Didn't matter. All that mattered now was ten grand.

"Get the fucking money, Tommy. Any fucking way you can."

* * *

The confessional window slid open.

"How long has it been since your last confession?"

"Coupla days."

"And what do you wish to confess?"

"Nothing. I've been pretty good. Over the last coupla days, I mean."

"Then why are we here, Tommy?"

"It's safe in here."

"If you've done nothing worthy of confession over the past couple of days, then why are we sitting here whispering in this box?"

"The thing you said last time. About the lion. Why did you say that?"

"It's scripture. I don't write it. I select it and recite it."

"I know. I mean why did you select that particular passage? What message were you trying to send?"

"The message that the world is unkind to the unthinking. If you meander about without a plan, without any kind of direction, without purpose, you'll find trouble."

"And why would you assume I have no plan or direction?"

"You're serious?"

"I'm not an idiot. You make me sound like the fourth Stooge."

"You know where you come from. You know where you are at this very minute. But where are you going? If you wander in the desert, prepare to be tempted, to endure hardships, to have your faith shaken."

"That's it? Just generic priest shit? Can we stop with the riddles in the name of God? Jesus Christ, padre. I don't have fucking time for puzzles..."

"Ahem."

"Sorry... I'm sorry. My God, Father, I've stepped into it this time."

"Well, here's more generic priest malarkey. Isaiah 6:8: Then I heard the voice of the Lord saying, 'Whom shall I send? And who will go for us?' And I said, 'Here am I. Send me!'"

"I heard a voice, believe me."

"But are you listening?"

"Busy at the moment, but I hope to up my volunteer activity real soon. Maybe I'll coach the church rec league or something."

"A bit from Daniel before I let you go: 'A stream of fire issued and came out from before him; a thousand thousands served him, and ten thousand times ten thousand stood before him; the court sat in judgment, and the books were opened.'"

Like I said, I didn't have time for puzzles.

* * *

When I was growing up, my old man, frustrated with my behavior and disappointed in me in general, decided it was time he taught me a lesson. He was tired, he said — tired of lecturing me, yelling at me, seeing me hang out with losers, hearing my mother say prayers for me as she lay in bed at night, having the nuns repeatedly drop by the house wondering why I wasn't in school, and having the cops bring me home at all hours of the night. But most of all, he was tired of beating my ass for all of the above.

One day, a truant officer showed up at my door, holding me by the collar. He had found me in a lot down off Fuhrman Boulevard, hiding behind a building smoking a cigarette when I was supposed to be in school. When he brought me home to turn me in to my old man, my father upon answering the door pushed me away and back into the arms of the officer.

"I don't want him. You take him away. Nothin' I say is getting through to him," my old man said. "Get him outta here."

My father walked back into the house and shut the door, leaving me in the custody of the truant officer. I was led back to the officer's car, put in the back seat and hauled downtown to the holding center on Franklin Street.

"Who do we have here?" said the desk sergeant as we walked through the door.

"Found him skipping school and his father doesn't want him," the officer said. "Instead, he told me to have his ass tossed in the can."

"We can arrange that," the sergeant said.

He looked over his shoulder and motioned to a fellow officer behind him. "Officer Carney, can you escort our friend in for processing?"

"My pleasure, Sarge."

I watched as the officer walked toward me, unsure what was happening.

"Please place your hands behind your back, young man."

My eyes suddenly were filled with tears, but I fought with all my might to make sure none fell.

Carney grabbed my hands, pulled his cuffs from his belt and snapped them around my wrists. They were tight and they pinched my skin. The officer walked me around to the other side of the desk and toward the back of the room, where he undid the cuffs and told me to place my hands on the counter in front of me.

"Please give me your index finger," he said firmly.

I did what he asked, and he proceeded to press each of my fingers, one-by-one, into a pad of ink and then onto a sheet of paper containing a series of square boxes labeled: thumb, first finger, second finger and so on...

Upon finishing, Carney walked me through a door to an empty room where he told me to strip down to nothing but my boxers. Taking my clothing and my shoes, he put the items in a box and handed me a one-piece orange jumpsuit. Then, he grabbed my arm and walked me down a narrow hallway with a cement wall on one side and iron cages on the other. The officer stopped in front of a cell with an old man sitting in the corner. He looked haggard, like a homeless wino you'd see sitting on the sidewalk against a storefront. Carney took his ring of keys from out of his pocket and opened the door to the wino's cell.

"You've got a roommate, Carl. Tommy, this is Carl. Carl, Tommy."

Carney guided me into the cell and then slammed the door shut. I stood there motionless, unable to take my eyes off the wino. Carl was looking at me, too. His eyes were sort of bulging and he had a troubling smirk on his face.

"What they got you in here for?"

I didn't answer.

"I ain't gonna bite. You can tell me."

I backed away, keeping my eyes on the wino but still refusing to answer. Finally, my legs bumped into a long bench connected to the wall and I sat down, my eyes remaining fixed on the old bum.

"Well, you ain't gotta answer me I guess. I can talk and you can listen. Sitting in here with no one to talk to can make a guy a little crazy. You end up talking to yourself. I swear, every time I come here I get a little crazier. Caged like an animal, alone with nothing but your thoughts.

"I bet you're some kind of thief or something," Carl said. "Too young to be a pervert. Too small and scrawny to be a killer. You're a little thief aren't ya? Yeah, that's what ya are — a fucking thief. I fucking know a thief when I see one. Well, ain't nothing to steal in here. Ain't no one got shit in here but their thoughts, and ya can't steal those. Even if ya could, ya probably wouldn't want them. Most of the thoughts people have in a place like this are fucking crazy."

I sat there for the next few hours, staring at my new friend and doing all I could to stay as far away as possible. Eventually, I heard the grating sound of the large metal hallway door being slid open. A few seconds later, the sergeant was standing outside the cell.

"Show the boy your leg, Carl."

Carl scooted down on his bunk so that both of his legs touched the floor. He grabbed his left calf with both hands and gave it a twist. Then he rolled up his jumpsuit to just above his knee and pulled his leg off entirely. With a smile, he held it in the air and pointed with his other hand to a hideous looking stump. It looked like the end of an extra-wide loaf of bread that had been pre-sliced a quarter way through and then dipped lightly in tomato sauce.

"There it is," Carl said, smiling. "They didn't do such a good job. Rich people's stubs don't look like this. Their doctors are better. But you get what you pay for, and since I ain't got any money anyway, mine got done for free."

I did everything in my power not to throw up.

"Tell him why you had to have your leg cut-off."

"Yeah, alright," Carl said. "Well, I got beat up by a bunch of thugs on the street. They stomped me pretty good. Leg was broken bad. Never had it looked at though. Gangrene set in and the infection spread. One day, I woke up in the hospital. Apparently, I had been found in the street. I don't remember. Anyway, they told me my leg had to come off. Guess it was for the best. Never worked since those guys stomped me anyway."

So, yeah, they were teaching me a lesson — trying to scare me straight. I didn't know it at the time. All I could think of was how badly I wanted to get the hell out of there. I wanted to cry. I never did, though. I already knew then, even at the age of 11, that you couldn't let anyone know when you were scared. Once someone finds out, they'll eat you alive. But, I was scared out of my fucking mind. And I wanted out.

After another hour spent in the cell alone with Carl, Carney appeared.

"Good news, kid. You posted bail."

He threw me my clothes, and after I dressed myself, Carney led me out of the cell and back to booking, where my father was waiting. The officer then undid my cuffs and pushed me toward my dad, who the desk sergeant had called to come pick me up.

"He's all yours."

We walked out of the station and south down Franklin toward the ward.

"Well, mister, wuddya think?"

I shrugged my shoulders and kept my head down, staring at the pavement beneath me.

"I dunno."

"You dunno? What do you mean you dunno?"

"I dunno."

"Well, here's what I know: you better shape up, 'cus if you don't, that's what the future has in store for ya."

My old man was a tough guy. He'd hardly been an angel himself. He was no stranger to the bottle or brawling in the street. He knew, too, what the inside of a cell looked like. He wasn't the smartest guy in the world, but he often knew what he was talking about. And that day, he was predicting my goddamn future, and he was dead on.

I guess his lesson didn't work.

CHAPTER FOUR

"Little more coffee, hon?"

"Just a little. Thanks." I'd had enough but was comfortable where I was sitting.

J.J.'s on Louisiana Street was a dump. Its white painted sign was fading. The inside was dingy from decades of slinging hash. The pleather stool seats along the counter were cracked. The linoleum floors were grimy. The cheap porcelain coffee cups were permanently stained from years of pouring coffee and pouring hearts.

I loved the joint.

I twirled a spoon around absently in my coffee despite the fact I take it black. What to do? What to do? I wasn't qualified to do anything straight that made more than ten bucks an hour or so. So forty hours a week at ten bucks an hour is four hundred bucks. If I finagled some overtime I might eek out five hundred. It would take twenty weeks of working at that rate to cover this nut. I don't fucking have twenty weeks. Shit, I might not even have twenty days.

I could find someone who needed a package delivered. That was never my thing but I had a pretty good idea where to find that kind of work. It might take only a trip or two across the border to make what I need. If I got pinched though, it would be game, set and match. It was a federal border. The Feds don't fuck around, and I sure as shit wasn't willing to test them. Then again, if I didn't come up with the money, I was a goner any way. Still, a decade or more in a federal penitentiary, at least to me, was a fate worse than death.

Nonetheless, it was either work like a mule or be a mule. Those seemed like the options. Move some rock or do some hard time in a hard place.

"Cammy," I said to the waitress, "whaddya suppose this place is worth?"

* * *

After leaving J.J's I caught a bus, hopped off at Abbott Road and cut through Cazenovia Park toward Seneca Street and then headed south to Greymount Avenue. When I reached the third house from the corner, I stopped and stood there on the sidewalk. No, I wasn't casing the joint. I was about to do something far more ballsy than breaking into the place: I was about to knock on the door. Wasn't anyone behind those walls who was going to be happy to see my sorry ass. But, there was someone inside that house who'd been on my mind a while.

I knocked on the door and heard a voice shout from inside.

"Just a minute!"

My stomach dropped. I was nervous as hell — a bad nervous.

The door opened and the woman on the other side looked at me, checked me up and down, and then sighed in exasperation.

"Tommy, goddamn it. Whaddy'a doing here?"

"You know why I'm here, Bette."

"Tommy you know Katie don't want you coming 'round. Goddamn you, Tommy. She's gonna go crazy when she finds out."

"You don't have to tell her, Bette. I was never here as far as you're concerned. Anyway, can I see him?"

"Oh Christ, Tommy, you ain't seen him in what now, a year-and-a-half? Goddamn it, why now?"

"You know I was away, Bette. And I know Katie told me to get lost. But that doesn't mean I haven't been thinking about him. And I know Katie's working right now, so she ain't gotta know about this. Ain't nobody gotta know."

"Goddamn it," Bette said again. She looked behind her, then looked back at me, rolled her eyes and threw her arms up in frustration. "Yeah, I guess… what the hell. Come in. Even a loser like you has the right to see his kid, I guess. Christ almighty, my daughter sure knows how to pick 'em. I thought I taught her better, but guess not."

I walked through the door and Bette pointed at my feet.

"Take your shoes off and follow me. You get dirt all over the floor and Katie will kill the both of us. He's back here in the living room. C'mon. He just woke up from a nap."

I followed Bette to the back of the house, through the kitchen and into the living room. Cartoons played on the television. Over the TV you could hear a little boy speaking gibberish in a little sing-songy voice. There he was, my son — Thomas Ronan Patton. My heart began to race and I could feel my eyes well up with tears. He was two years old, but I hadn't seen him before I went away to county.

I walked over to where he was playing. He had his back turned to me and hadn't seen me yet. I sat down on the floor and scooted toward him, softly laying my hand on his back. He looked over his left shoulder and smiled.

"Hey buddy," I said softly. My God, he was beautiful. "It's your daddy."

I could see Bette roll her eyes. "Daddy… yeah, right. Father, yes, but I don't know about Daddy."

I ignored her and kept my eyes fixed on Thomas. His dark brown eyes looked like Hershey kisses. His grin expanded and I removed a small drop of spittle from his lower lip with my knuckle.

"How ya' doing pal? Whaddy'a have there? Blocks?"

He handed me the block in his hand and then reached down and picked up another off the floor. He held it up to show me and then touched the block in my hand with the one in his.

I couldn't take my eyes off him. I held his hand and pulled it toward my face and kissed it. I didn't know what to say. I didn't want to say anything. I just wanted to stare at him. And I couldn't help but hate myself for missing out on every second of his life these past eighteen months.

I looked at Bette.

"He's really something else," she said, smiling.

I had so much I wanted to ask; about Thomas, about Katie, and about whether there was any chance I could somehow be a part of their lives again. But I couldn't bring myself to speak. And, really, I had no business asking about anything. I had done nothing to demonstrate that I deserved any answers to any questions about their lives. I had demonstrated only that I did not deserve to be a part of them. And besides, I knew the answers and had no interest in hearing them, despite their truth.

I spent about twenty minutes with Thomas, just playing with him and his blocks, looking at him, imagining what he'd become and wondering whether I'd be around to see it.

Finally, at some point, I heard Bette say, "She'll be here pretty soon. You should probably go."

I took a deep breath and again felt my eyes water. I rubbed Thomas's back and then leaned forward and kissed his cheek.

"I have to go, buddy. I love you."

I pushed myself up and walked out of the living room and through the kitchen. Before turning the corner toward the front of the house, I looked back at Thomas. He was watching me leave. He smiled at me and waved his hand. I smiled, waved back and tried as hard as I could not to lose it.

"I'll see you soon, buddy," I said.

But, really, I wondered to myself whether I'd ever see him again. Or anyone else for that matter.

* * *

"J" was a small Indian guy. Maybe Pakistani, but I think Indian. I should know, as I've chatted with him over coffee and hash (the corned beef variety) a thousand times. He was one of the two Js in "J.J.'s." His brother, also called 'J,' died a few years back. One day he just wasn't there. Gone without a trace.

"He's died," was all J said. End of story. The show went on without him but the buzz wasn't quite the same.

"J it's good to see you. You haven't been around as much."

"I'm there most of the time. It's you who has not been around."

"Well I was just there the other day. Cammy told me I could come see you."

"She called me. I thought we had been robbed. Again."

"You've been robbed?"

"Twice. I think I know by whom but they did not get much money. They probably needed it more than me."

"Must be a Hindu thing. I'd kill 'em."

"My generosity does not extend to my home. I will put a hole in your face here," he said with a little smile but a lot of sincerity as he pointed between his eyes.

"I'm not here to rob you. My reputation must precede me."

"You're not a thief."

"Actually, I kind of am a thief. Well, no… actually, I'm a total thief."

"A burglar is not a thief. Know the difference. One is about stuff. One is about honor." He went on, "You're a good tipper. And you leave your spot clean when you go. I notice the little things."

"I may be a bum, but I ain't a slob."

"Jail requires a level of organization and tidiness. Like the military. It's all about routine."

"True. You don't want the stuff you don't got all over the place."

"So, what can I do for you?"

"Obviously you know a bit about me. I've done time. I'm no saint. I've made bad decisions. But I'm not a bad guy."

"I agree. People say it is so. Even strangers."

"Strangers?" What the hell did that mean?

"So why are you here?"

The 'strangers' comment threw me. Was everyone talking about me?

"I think you need a business partner, and I know just the guy."

"Let me guess. It is you?'

"Yes. I'm on the straight and narrow. I've got a kid now. He's two. I want to see him grow up without bars in between us."

"He might say the same about you if he could talk."

"I don't want him to think I'm a fuckup. I want to grind it out and do things right."

"One cup of coffee at a time, eh?"

"Exactly."

"As my brother used to say, 'you've got to break a few eggs to make an omelet.' He loved that expression. I'm not sure he knew what it meant but that's okay. I've found people in America often say things they don't understand. Repeatedly."

"I can see how you'd come to that conclusion. And I know I've said I've gone straight in the past, if that's what you're getting at. But now…"

"You mean it. I believe you. What type of partnership do you envision?"

"The kind that starts with you loaning me ten grand or my next stop is to the life insurance agent."

"How about I loan you this money and you still go to the agent? Make me the beneficiary. It's collateral for me. Incentive for you."

"You're like some kind of Gangster Gandhi."

"I am a businessman. Not a priest. You've got one of those already."

* * *

The crows were gathered en masse on the staircase in front of my place, cawing and jockeying for position. I picked up a stick from the lawn of the apartment next store and hurled it at the porch, purposely hitting the bottom stairs so that the sound would scare them away. Most dispersed but there were a few stragglers, so I raced up the sidewalk and shooed the rest. As they flew off, I could see a rolled up newspaper on the porch. Inside was a dead fish — now with a large gaping whole in the middle of its body, courtesy of the crows.

As a fan of The Godfather, I immediately understood the

message sent by Mr. Carlo Della Pina: either pay up or prepare to be sleeping with the fishes. Hardly subtle. And if that message wasn't ominous enough, it was underscored by the murder of crows — a sign my people associate with impending death.

"I've seen The Godfather, Francis Ford Coppola!" I shouted to nobody in particular and everyone in general. "You know Fish from Barney Miller was the one that delivered the fish in the movie. Get it? Fucking idiots!"

I took a seat on the steps, lit a cigarette, reached behind me, grabbed the newspaper and tossed the fish on the sidewalk in front of me. As I stared down at it, I imagined my own lifeless body floating atop the Niagara River, maybe with my throat slit ear-to-ear or, perhaps, a hole in the back of my head. For my sake, I hoped it was the latter. I'd just wash ashore as some little black kids were trying to snag sheephead carp at the foot of Porter Street along the rocks of the river near the Peace Bridge. They're mostly dead too, even when they're still alive. The carp, I mean.

If it happens, I hope it's quick. I hope I don't see it coming: alive one second, dead the next and never the wiser. I know that some in Carlo's line of work aren't content with just a simple hit. There is no joy for them in a quick finality. They usually prefer to send a message — a long, drawn out, bloody and torturous message. They want the word to spread across the underworld that failure to live up to the end of a bargain won't be tolerated. Actions speak loudly in Mr. Della Pina's business. And every now and then, Carlo's been known for his over-reactions.

* * *

The Cadillac was parked in front of the house.

"Get in," my dapper stranger said. "Let's go for a ride."

I thought for a second. I could run, but I'm no O.J. I could charge, but I've only got a blade and he's got who knows what. And, oh yeah, he's probably very experienced in the killing department.

So I got in.

"Nice to see you again…"

"I'm fucking starved. Let's grab some eggs and coffee. I know just the perfect place."

"You fattening the calf? A last meal kind of thing?"

He laughed, and it felt genuine. Not sinister or ironic.

"Unless the cholesterol gets you, it's unlikely this will be your last meal. You can call me 'Tip', by the way, and I'm buying."

"Tip and Tommy Get a Coffee. Sounds like a Goo-Goo Dolls tune. Just another morning in the Buff."

"Indeed. New research suggests that breakfast is not, in fact, the most important meal of the day. Turns out an ad company planted that seed and we've been reflexively playing it back ever since. It's really just another meal. Mass fucking media, ya know what I'm sayin?"

"Advertising will be the death of us."

"Not all of us," he said without the trace of a grin. "Some of us will die unnaturally, violently even. The statistics are clear. It's not a matter of race but of class. You can be any color and hail from anywhere. If you're born into a well off family, you're likely to do all right. But if you're lily white and born into a shanty-Irish, piece of shit family..."

"You get driven to J.J.'s in a Cadillac."

The car pulled in front of J.J.'s.

"Breakfast of champions awaits. Don't be scared. Fear impairs your judgment. You need to exercise good judgment today. There you go. That's your fortune for the day. I'm full service."

Cammy 'greeted' us at the door. She wasn't her saucy self.

"They're in the booth in the back."

As we walked to the back, I could feel the blood drain from my face. There was the priest sitting with J.

"What the fuck?"

"Over easy, Tommy?"

"You read me like a book, Padre."

"The Good Book."

* * *

My old man's been in the ground for almost fifteen years now. My mom, meanwhile, wants nothing to do with me. She gave up on me, said I'm no good and that I've put her through enough. She's still keeping tabs though, getting the skinny on me from Father Frank. Last time I was inside, he was a regular visitor — one of my only ones. My mother has long used him as her crying rag, someone on whom she could dump her laundry list of complaints about me; someone whom she could ask where she had gone wrong; someone to whom she could wonder whether I'd ever change and, yeah, someone she would pester and beg to pray for me.

I'm not sure whether any of that praying has done any good. Maybe it has, I dunno. I mean, shit, I'm not dead yet. But it certainly hasn't kept me from being locked up, and it hasn't kept me outta trouble either. And shit, I was in some big-ass trouble now.

If my mother only knew who Father Frank was keeping company with, she'd probably want nothing to do with him. If only she could see the Padre now. This wasn't a fucking church group gathered in the back of J.J.'s. If a man is really known by the kind of company he keeps, then there wouldn't be anything good to know about Father Frank based on the group he was hanging with at the moment. A lot of bad seeds.

"Great to see you again, Father," said Tip, reaching to shake the priest's hand.

"Tip," Father Frank nodded. "It's nice to see you too."

"You two know each other?" I asked incredulously.

"I've ministered to Tip," the priest said, staring at Tip with a knowing smirk. "Surely you weren't under the impression that you were my only customer, Tommy. Guys like me — we have a flock, you know. It's like anything. You need to diversify."

"Excuse me for saying so, Father, but maybe I'm not the only one who's been wandering in the desert."

The priest smiled.

"Your concern for me is heartening, Tommy. Your profession notwithstanding, I always knew there was a selflessness in you. And while we are airing our concerns, let me remind you of Proverbs: He who conceals his sins does not prosper, but whoever confesses and renounces them finds mercy."

"Are you talking about me or you, Father?"

He did not reply.

Maybe he had nothing to say. Or maybe there was nothing he could say.

"Father," Tip said solemnly, looking Frank dead in the eye, "the seal has been broken. It's out of my hands now."

"Between us, I think Revelation is shite. Mularkey. But

I understand your larger point. You have bought us time. Your sins are absolved, from my perspective. 'Neither a borrower nor a lender be'."

"That's Shakespeare, not God," I piped up.

"Is there a difference?"

"Tip, I asked you for time and you've given it. I thank you. And our mutual acquaintance thanks you too. Well, if he doesn't thank you, he won't kill you anyway."

"Hallelujah. I'm out." Tip deadpanned looking to heaven, hands wide. With that, he got up and left.

"I must be going myself," J said. He then pointed to the priest's breakfast and said, "that is on the house."

"What the fuck are you two gabbing on and on about?" I asked impatiently.

"Tip ran into some trouble at the Track over in Fort Erie. Went long on something he should not have."

"Happens," I said.

"To some more than others. He came to me for advice. Told me he was going to do some contract work for quick cash. Through careful attention to detail and deductive reasoning I was able to divine, even through the partition, that your name was on his list."

"What the fuck?"

"So I made him a deal. I took from the coffers the cash

so he could get level. He's paying me back in weekly install-
ments."

"My head hurts."

"And the 'interest' payment was he was to leave you
alone while I figured out a plan to help you. Which I have."

"So, wait then: you know what this debt is all about that
I owe? What the fuck, care to share those details with me?"

"Mr. Tip did not offer that information up to me. Knowing you, and knowing his line of work, I just assumed those details were between you two gentlemen. That's not my business.
My only role here is simple: to buy some time and make sure
you stay alive."

"I don't care if they'll kill me. You're not going to fuck
me, Padre."

His tone, which had been somewhat grave, lightened.

"You fucked yourself, Tommy. I'm unfucking you if
there is such a thing."

"Why me?"

"She moves in mysterious ways."

My head was throbbing now. Why was everyone talking
in riddles? Most people in this fucking shithole of a neighborhood had trouble with just basic English let alone word play like
these guys were all doing.

"And what the fuck are you doing shooting the shit with

the Haji? Since when are you two running mates?" I was equal parts bewildered and angry. My voice got unnaturally high in spots. It was like I was in Grammar school again.

"It's a non-denominational relationship. We share thoughts from time to time on current events, matters of the faith, those of the flesh…"

"Maybe he was a priest in a former life."

"Maybe. One thing about Hinduism I find so moving, and I don't pretend to be an expert by any stretch, is this idea of doing it right or having to do it again. I don't know if I can believe with their letter of the law, but I do agree with its spirit."

My vision wasn't blurring, but it was getting a little out of focus. My motherboard was shutting down.

"We must all find tremendous urgency to get things right. I prefer to do it in this life as I'm not convinced there's another. Our tradition is you've got to get right with The Lord if you're to move on to the afterlife. It's not about lifetimes ago. It's about evening the ledger of this life. And this life is finite. None of us knows how much of it we're given."

He leaned in.

"Some of us do know," he said with hushed gravity, "that the hourglass has been turned over."

CHAPTER FIVE

The walls had come down. Living in grey Buffalo must lead people to see things in black and white; those feel like the only colors available to you. But now this: Am I intuitively dyslexic, where good guys are really bad and bad guys actually good? Was everyone a fetid grey mess of both? Or was there more to the spectrum that I'd never been exposed to but now, after more than twenty years pounding the pavement, I was finally seeing?

Amazing Grace: was blind, but now I see.

"Another," I said too brusquely.

"Another three bucks," she countered in kind.

I handed over the money. She handed over the beer. I reached over and grabbed a small black pepper shaker off the bar. I'd seen the old-timers do this but I'd never tried it in any of the (what, millions?) beers I'd downed. But today was an exceptional day. I put two good shakes in and watched the flecks gently sink down, making their way to the bottom of the glass. It was supposed to keep the head, undoubtedly bullshit, but this head wouldn't be long enough to be observed for the curative powers of black pepper. In one long draw, I drained it dry.

"Same way."

I reached for the three bucks in my coat pocket.

"Next time," she said, with the slightest glint of recognition that I was a man in need of a drink if ever there was one.

I smiled at her. "Today is like that episode of Seinfeld where everything is its opposite. You know, the one where George tells the truth about how pathetic his life really is and still ends up picking up the hot blonde at the diner?"

Her expression couldn't have been more transparent if she had a 'WTF' carved on her forehead.

"Like Opposite Day on Sponge Bob?"

"Never mind. Thanks for the beer."

I grabbed a napkin and asked her for a pen. I needed to graph the day's events in order to wrap my head around it all:

Mom fucking priest.

Priest gambling.

Killer confesses he's going to kill me.

Priest running misdirection with Ma and hit man.

And an Indian coffee shop owner.

Ma fucking priest.

* * *

First came the bag. Then, I was Gilloolied like Nancy

Kerrigan.

I was walking down Seneca Street on my way to get my morning coffee when out of nowhere, a black cinch bag was pulled over my head. The drawstring was tightened. Before I could shout, a baseball bat smashed against both of my knees. The pain was unspeakable. I hadn't even hit the sidewalk before the second blow — this time with the bat's butt end — slammed into my face, right between the eyes. Within seconds, my mouth was filled with blood. I was then shoved into the backseat of a car. I could hear over my own loud gasps the tires squeal as we sped away from the curb. Someone was sitting in back with me. They had one hand around my neck, holding my left shoulder, and the other clutching my right arm. Then a fist was buried into my gut. I doubled over and choked on the blood now clogging my throat.

"Shut the fuck up, asshole!" ordered a voice I did not recognize.

I could feel the car turning corners and then speeding straight ahead — turning and speeding, turning and speeding. Some ten minutes later, we stopped and I was pulled from the car. My knees gave out. Hands grabbed my jacket at both shoulders, and I was dragged over pavement while I continued to gag and cough. I was then tossed on the ground. By then, I knew we were inside a building. I could sense a change in the air, and the ground I was now laying upon was cooler and smoother.

The bag was pulled off my head. It took a few seconds before I could focus my eyes, but once I did, I recognized the face staring down at me.

"Hey, how ya doing, Sunshine? You don't look so good."

It was Tip.

He reached down and pulled me up, holding me from underneath the arms. He dragged me over to a booth and tossed my limp body onto the cushioned bench seat. A cloth napkin was tossed on top of me.

"Clean yourself up, Tommy. And sit up. It's bad manners to slouch at the table. Didn't they teach you any fucking manners growing up in the Ward?"

I struggled to push myself up, but finally managed. I removed the napkin from my face and looked at the person sitting across from me. My heart skipped a beat and then sank.

"Welcome to Lackawanna, Thomas," Carlo Della Pina said. "I appreciate you taking time out of your schedule to meet with me. Tip, how about bringing our friend here some coffee. As I understand it, he never got a chance to have a cup this morning."

I swallowed the blood in my throat, sat up straight and patted my nose with the napkin to make sure I didn't bleed on the tablecloth.

"Mr. Della Pina…"

"Please. Call me Carlo."

"Carlo. OK. Carlo. I'm sorry. I'm told I owe you money but I gotta be honest, I don't recall ever doing any business with you, sir. I never placed any bets with anyone out here either. I would remember. Honest. And you ain't someone I'd skip out on; I'm not that stupid."

"You're right, Tommy. Well, you're half right. We didn't do any business. But here's where you're wrong: you are stupid. Let me educate you. See, I know it was you who did the Carmody job."

"Carmody? Carlo, I don't know what you're talking about. Honest."

"See, this is what I mean. You're stupid. Actually, you're even more stupid than I thought because now you are lying to my face. Listen, Tommy, don't fuck with me. I'll put a hole right through your fucking eye as we sit here, you piece of shit. I'm giving you a chance."

I didn't say anything. There was nothing to say. Jimmy Carmody was a South Buffalo bookie. I had done business with him a few times. He was an older guy, and so, in my mind, he was low-hanging fruit. He made his books in the back room of a minimart off South Park. I learned his patterns and knew that on certain nights, he'd be in the store alone after closing. So, one night I waited things out, and when he was inside alone, I broke in and robbed him of more than $4,000. You see, J was wrong. I am a robber, too.

Anyway, it was a perfect job.

Though, over time, some bad bets ate up most of the haul, I never attracted any heat. But my line of work isn't two-dimensional. It's more like an eight-sided dice. Like a stone thrown in a pond, there's a ripple effect. I've never been one to worry much about those ripples. But the ripple effect from the Carmody job — unbeknownst to me until now — turned out to be larger than I ever could have anticipated. And now, I had a lot to worry about because, as Carlo explained to me, the ripple had reached his waters.

"After you hit Carmody, he had trouble making pay-ments," Carlo said. "He eventually came to me and I agreed to keep him afloat. As you know, there were a lotta people he owed. Lotta angry people. Before he could make good, and more importantly, before he could pay me back, he got whacked. You were in county when that happened. I know that wasn't you. But whoever it was took whatever he had. Jimmy's no longer around. But his debts remain. So, the way I see it, the person responsible for his debts has to pick up that burden. And that person is you. You were the cause of his problems; now, you fix 'em. I don't care what Jimmy owed other people. I only care about what he owed me. And factoring interest, I figure I have ten grand coming my way. You got until the 28th. How you get that money is your concern and your problem. I don't give a shit what you have to do. But you better get it, or else — and I promise you this — you're gonna get it. And when that happens, the bag will cover more than just your head."

How Carlo found out it was me who robbed Jimmy, I don't know. Maybe Katie, who always had her suspicions, went to the cops. But the cops did business with Jimmy too — something they knew I knew. Bringing me in threatened them. But once Carmody got knocked off and the cops knew their payday wasn't coming, maybe they ratted me to Carlo as their way of bringing me to justice. Who knows?

Carlo motioned to Tip.

"Have the boys see to it that Mr. Patton leaves Lackawanna."

Tip reached into the booth, grabbed me by the arm and waved over the men who had been kind enough to personally escort me from South Buffalo to Lackawanna for my meeting with Mr. Della Pina this morning. They pushed me out to the car, this time sans the cinch bag, and shoved me into the backseat. Upon driving into South Buffalo, they pulled off the road and behind a vacant warehouse off Seneca Street.

They pulled me from the car and walked me over to the

warehouse wall. Then, they spent a good forty-five seconds using me as a heavy bag.

I fell to the ground, again gasping for air.

"The 28th, douchebag," said one of my escorts. And then he put an exclamation on that friendly reminder with a boot to my ribs.

I lay there for several minutes bruised, battered and bleeding. I felt like death, but I was still alive. Murphy's Law notwithstanding, it was always better to look on the bright side.

* * *

"Jesus, Mary and Joseph! Who's done a tap dance on your face?"

I just wanted to be held more so than any other time I could remember.

"Wrong number," I deadpanned. "Listen, I know you don't want to see me. I get it. I won't take but five minutes of your time. Just hear me out and I'm out the door."

"I'm listening. Start talking. I've got to get home so my mother can get going. She told me you stopped by, in case you're wondering. He's your son. It's your right. But don't make a habit of it. And don't come by looking like this."

"Believe me. I won't." As much as this thaw with the only woman I ever really loved was as uplifting as it was unexpected, the dead last thing in the world I needed right now was more emotional shit. I was all stocked up in that department.

"Let me give you the… what the fuck do you call those things?"

"What things?"

"They're books—but just the important parts."

"Cliff notes?"

"Right. Cliff notes. Let me give you them. Alright, follow me here. And I'm sorry for dumping this on you but anyway… There's a guy that's going to whack me by the 28th. Actually, on the 28th in all likelihood. So, I want to get an insurance policy before then so that when that happens you'll get some money for my boy. Our boy."

"Why is someone going to kill you?"

Here, I would have liked a little more concern. She was a little too matter-of-fact about it for my liking, maybe because she really knew the reason why, or maybe because she didn't care. In fact, maybe she was surprised someone hadn't already. Either way, I guess she had just run out of the ability to give a fuck.

"Not important. I stole something from somebody who then couldn't pay this other guy back and then someone else— not me—killed that guy, so now the other guy is making me pay him back… It's convoluted. Regardless, I'm trapped in this clusterfuck."

"How much?"

"Ten grand. May as well be a million."

"You ask your Ma?"

"Doubt she has a pot to piss in or a window to throw it out of. Besides, there's 'tension' there right now."

"How come? You're all she's got."

"That's what I thought too. Turns out we were wrong."

"Good for her. Everybody deserves somebody — or in my case, somebody else."

I let the dig pass. "People are getting what they deserve all over the place it seems. Anyway, I need his Social so I can name him on the policy."

"I'm not giving you his Social. Who the fuck knows what you'll do with it." Now she was using that incredibly irritated tone of hers that I was way too familiar with. It was oddly comforting.

"What the fuck am I gonna do with it? Do you honestly think I'm that big a cocksucker to identity theft my own kid? Really?"

"Yes. Yes, I do. You wouldn't do it on purpose. You'd do it because you're so fucking lazy. It's like Cliff Notes. You're the human version. You're always cutting corners instead of doing anything the hard way; the right way."

"Very deep, Oprah. But if you'll just give me the number I'll put it on the form, deliver the policy to you, and when you read about my untimely end in the paper you can cash it in."

"That's all you've got? Get an insurance policy and wait for them to show up? Can't you at least be a clever crook? There's no way out of this? Zero? None?"

"I'm all ears. Thought about buying J.J.'s but that's a lot of coffee and eggs by the 28th." I turned and headed away. This wasn't happening. And as comforting as it may have been to hear her lecture me like the old days, I didn't have the time.

"Where are you going?"

"I've got to see the priest."

"Final confession?"

"Yes. His."

CHAPTER SIX

Katie was right. I was lazy. Dying was the easy way out. Living was going to take work, and I ain't ever been much for work, at least in the traditional sense of the word. Crime paid better. And even despite the need that I had to finally go straight given that my next stop on the fuck-up train was state prison, I no longer had enough time for legitimacy. My expiration date was approaching.

I had only two options: Be clever, as Katie suggested; or be lazy and let them come and get me, which Katie accused me of doing and probably secretly wanted. Yet her tone said otherwise.

That Katie would berate me for "cutting corners" — while deserved — was somewhat baffling. What interest could she possibly have in me still being around? She didn't want any part of me, and she didn't want me in our boy's life, either. She'd be far better off with me dead, especially with Thomas named as the beneficiary of my life insurance policy. But, the fact that she wouldn't provide our son's Social Security number underscored what a scumbag she really thinks I am. I realize this was entirely my fault. But still, the more I thought about how Katie firmly believed that I would fuck over our son, the more pissed off it made me and the more convinced I was that it was she who went to the cops about Carmody. This woman who once loved me now absolutely despised me.

She was just like my old lady.

When I was a boy, my mother called me her "prionsa," which is Gaelic for "prince." I was her sunshine. She adored me.

But now, like Katie, she wanted nothing to do with me. I was her greatest disappointment. I was a blight on her family. I was no good. I was a "prionsa" non grata.

I had no other choice but to accept Katie's disgust with me. Harder to come to terms with, however, was my mother's. That's not to say I couldn't understand. Still, I could not help but feel a sense of abandonment, no matter how deserving that abandonment was. Lower than a no-good crook was a mother who walked away from her own kid.

Harder to accept, too, was that my mother's only solace from the pain I caused her was found in the arms of priest, whose vow of chastity was being broken between the legs of a woman I had always considered to a be a saint.

* * *

"Pressure makes diamonds."

"Well then I'll be shining from here to kingdom come, ma. I guess you've got me wrapped around your finger like a diamond ring."

"You weren't getting the message on your own."

"I need a fucking drink."

"That's exactly what you do not need. You need your wits about you now." She leaned forward in her chair and kind of lowered her head as if in prayer. It was meditative. "When you were born you laughed all the time. You never cried. You were talking in full sentences before you were two years old. So much promise. When you were a teenager you got into some trouble but that was more about the neighborhood than about you. You were still good at heart. When your father died I felt sure you'd turn around and bend toward The Lord and the light."

"Like you've done now, evidently."

She lunged forward like a cobra and hit me hard with an open hand across the face.

"And where's that fucking mouth of yours gotten you, huh? Jail. No girl. No job. No future. A son you don't even fucking know. And now, possibly, an early grave. And you question my motives? How dare you. You only understand the hammer. And now it's come down."

I leaned back in the chair; sure each of her five knotted fingers could be seen clearly outlined in red on my pasty white face but I'd survive. Wasn't the first time she's left an imprint of her fist in my mug.

The priest spoke, seated to my left in the purple upholstered chair that was my father's favorite. The fucking nerve.

"The Church too has lost its way. It's like a corporation. It's big, bloated, and its motives are clouded by lust for money. We've forgotten our mission. We've forgotten our purpose. Our purpose is to tend to the flock. We've become a Shepherds' Union. That's no good."

I wanted so badly to call bullshit on both this hypocritical motherfucker and his sanctimonious sermon. The balls of this guy. Yet I was overwhelmed. Overwhelmed by the situation. Panicked by the danger. Intrigued by the idea. I had one more stupid idea of my own to try first.

"As you now know, your mother and I have become close in recent years. What began as me tending to her as a pastor led to friendship and eventually more. Much more. Don't think I do not know what you're thinking. I do. You'd probably like nothing more than to break my neck. The hypocrite. The intruder. The…" He trailed off as if looking for a word that should exist but doesn't.

"We are where we are. All of us," she said. "None is perfect. None is an angel. We're all flesh and blood. We get one life and it's to be lived. We must do the best we can. That's all we're trying to do for you. I am your mother. Father is your spiritual guide. This is the test, the baptism by fire, we've all known would come. It's here and it's not gonna go away, Tommy. And it's a test you cannot cheat. But we will make certain you survive this. It's a test we will win. God as my witness."

"Tell me again how it will work," I said.

* * *

Pressure makes diamonds. Maybe the old lady was trying to tell me something. It is, after all, a mother's duty to guide her child. Perhaps she was actually trying to guide me out of the mess I've made.

With that possibility in mind, I dropped by Hanlon Jewelers on the corner of Abbott and Dorrance. The shop was a family business, now run by Gerry Hanlon who took over some twenty years ago for his old man who founded the business. Gerry was in his late sixties and the shop was really all he had. His wife had died a few years earlier after a brief battle with cancer and their only son, who was younger than me, was killed in a car crash in the early 1990s. Gerry definitely had his share of tough times, but that fact only made him like most everyone else who hailed from the Ward.

The store was empty when I walked in, save for the guy behind the counter. It wasn't Gerry, so I asked where the old man was.

"He's out running errands. I'm his nephew."

"He due back soon?"

"Probably an hour or so. Anything I can help you with?"

"Well, I had talked to Gerry a few days ago," I lied. "Told him I was going to drop by to check on some engagement rings. Time I made an honest woman out of my girlfriend. She's been up my ass. You know how it is."

"Yeah, we all fall eventually," the nephew said.

I was trying to buy myself time as I cased out the shop. I asked to see some rings to keep the nephew talking as I spied the lay of the land. After about ten minutes, I asked whether there was a restroom. The nephew pointed me to the back of the store.

"Go through that door there and first room on your right is a bathroom."

"Thanks."

As I walked toward the head, I scoped the room. I then entered the bathroom and closed the door behind me. Jackpot. There, on the wall facing me, was a window. I walked over to the toilet and flushed it, then turned the sink's faucet on to make it sound like I was using the facilities. I grabbed the latch on the window and lifted and turned it to the open position. I then nudged the screen off its track so that when I came back later at night, I would be able to easily move it out of my way. I pulled the window back down slowly, leaving the latch up so that it remained open. As long as the old man didn't check it at closing time, I was set.

Returning to the front of the store, I walked up to the counter.

"I think I have a better idea of what I'm after," I told the nephew. "Thanks for your help. I'm close to making a decision. I'll be back in a few days. Tell Gerry I'll give him a call."

"Fantastic. What's the name?"

"McMahon," I said. "Joey McMahon."

***

With a duffle bag, gloved hands and a ski mask, I returned to Hanlon's just before 2 a.m. I don't recall ever being so calm pulling a job. Maybe that's because there was little downside. If I got busted, I'd go to prison. But the upside was if I went to prison I wouldn't end up dead in a trunk with my dick in my mouth, courtesy of Carlo Della Pina.

I walked behind the building and pushed in the screen. Easy-peasy just as I had planned. I then slid the window open and used the sill to boost myself up and into the bathroom. I opened the bathroom door and stepped into the shop. The place had a pretty simple layout and with the light from the bathroom shining into the store the path leading behind the counter was lit better than I had expected.

But there was something else I didn't expect, and that

was the old man being inside the store at two in the morning. Apparently, some nights, he sleeps in the backroom and this was one of those nights.

Murphy's Law.

"Who the hell is here!" he screamed as he rushed from the back of the building into the shop. "Who the hell is here? I'll blow your fucking head off!"

I stopped cold in my tracks and crouched down behind the counter. I was no longer calm. In fact, it felt like my heart was about to burst through my chest.

Gerry rushed toward the counter. He knew I was there, but I was able to surprise him anyway before he could take his first step behind the counter. I jumped out from where I was crouched and appeared straight in his path. He was armed with a shotgun and his face was awash in fear. His arms shook wildly as he raised the gun to his chest. As horrified as I was, I could immediately sense his nervousness and without thinking, I rushed toward Gerry and clothes lined him. He fell to the ground and I kicked the shotgun from his hands. I thought for a second to grab it and blast a hole in his chest. Yet despite the insanity that engulfed the moment, a flash of clarity managed to find its way into my thought process and I decided against picking up the gun. I was a thief. I was no killer. That much I knew.

I raced back to the bathroom. Gerry scrambled to get

back on his feet. I hurried to the window and jumped out, hopping a fence and running through a series of residential backyards with the empty duffle bag in my hand and my face still masked.

I had no idea where I was headed, but I kept running.

Dogs barked.

And then I heard a single shotgun blast.

I was still alive, but for how long, I wasn't sure.

CHAPTER SEVEN

"Need a lift?"

Ordinarily, seeing Tip in this particular circumstance would be categorized as "negative." Whether owing to the fact that the old man could be just around the corner with his twenty-gauge, or my heart was pounding so much I thought I might croak to death by cock ingestion, I strangely welcomed the sight of the meticulous Cadillac.

"Love one. Trying to get in shape. Maybe bit off more than I can chew. I'll get back at it tomorrow."

I opened the door and slid into the front seat of the car. We started heading down Abbott Road. There was an unsettling air in the car this time. We drove for several miles before I finally tried to break the silence.

"Funny how you always seem to be there when I need a ride," I said, trying to lighten the mood. "You wouldn't be following me or anything, would you?"

"Yeah, well, I heard the starting gun go off," Tip said, keeping his eyes fixed on the road.

"Damn kids and their firecrackers."

Tip looked over at me, his face more serious than I had ever seen.

"Listen, Jerkoff. Listen good. You've got two options. I'm going to kill you for the wiseguy or I'm going to help you for the priest. No fucking faggot jeweler is going to get what's mine one way or the other."

"I have had a really long couple of days. Can we get a drink or is that against regulations?"

We pulled into the lot behind the Shebeen, an Irish gin mill that catered to underage suburban white kids. At this time of night it was dead. Must have been a school night.

"So the killing me part I'm clear on. Tell me about door number two."

"The priest likes you. I like the priest. He's asked me to do what I can do to keep you in the game as long as possible."

"The kicking my ass till my nose bled the other night, that was part of 'the game'?"

"Righto. Nobody can have any doubt I'll waste you in a hot second. And they shouldn't, 'cause quite frankly I will. Don't forget that for a second. But if I can get you out of this mess before that happens and still profit, I'm open to that too."

"OK. I'm open to ideas. So far I had robbing the jeweler. Your turn."

"What about the coffee shop? That's another thing your guardian angel put together. What about that?"

"What about it? I'm happy to go straight and pour coffee and sling hash for the rest of my days. But I can't make ten grand in the time I have. I need a bigger score."

"Maybe not. Maybe you're not looking at it the right way. Maybe the proceeds from breakfast can't get you there. Maybe there's another way."

"Fine. Done. Let's do it."

"Priest won't go for that nor will the Paesan. I have a devil on one shoulder and an angel on the other and they're both shaking their head 'no.' What about the insurance proposal the towel-head put on the table. What about that?"

"I'm a slow-learner. How does that help? When I get killed, he'll be flush with chutney or whatever-the-hell he eats. Carlo still has no money. I'm still dead. What am I missing?"

"Maybe you're not dead. Maybe you're reborn as some-one else. Isn't that what they think anyhow?"

"Are you saying what I think you're saying?"

"That's right," said Tip. "You die, but you really don't, know what I'm saying here?"

"Fake my death?"

"In a few days, we'll roll away the stone and off you go. Same guy new name. Something like that. Cause your name is mud right now. And mine is too if you don't turn up dead one way or the other. I'm strongly suggesting you consider the other. That fucking dot on his head might be from thinking. He's smart. Crafty in a quiet way. But I wouldn't fuck with him either. I have zero doubt he'd whack his own brother."

* * *

And so it came down to this: Keep on hustling and possibly end up dead, or fake my death in order to keep living.

The thought intrigued me — at least the way in which Tip explained: "Maybe you're reborn…"

Reborn. What an interesting concept. Rebirth, a new beginning, a clean slate: maybe this was my opportunity to not only do it all over, but do it right, too. But going down this path also meant permanent loss — most importantly, the loss of my son. There would be no turning back if I chose to be reborn because deciding to do so meant saying goodbye forever to the only life I've ever known.

"Look, let's say I agree to go along with this; I have to make sure my son is taken care of. I went and saw his mother about taking out a plan on myself and she refused to give me our kid's Social Security number because, in her mind, I'm such a fucking scum bag that I'd even stoop so low as to steal my own son's identity to somehow benefit myself. That's fucking crazy, by the way. But if I'm going to fake my own death, I need to make sure he's provided for and I don't see how making J my beneficiary is going to address that issue."

"You know your kid ain't my problem," Tip said. "But that said, you're worth more to me alive than dead right now, so in the name of the great American tradition of looking out for number one, I will make sure your son and his mom get paid in wake of your imaginary demise."

"I don't want you going near my family."

"You ain't got a choice."

"I believe in the right to die."

"That's good, cuz I can make that happen."

"Yes, both you and your henchmen have made that quite clear."

"Good. I'm glad there's no misunderstanding then," Tip said. "Time is winding down. Do the right thing, Tommy."

"That ain't ever been my strong point."

"Like they say, kid: No better time than the present."

CHAPTER EIGHT

"In my country, we think of rebirth as a bad thing. It's like repeating a test you don't score well enough on to pass."

"I know exactly what you mean." I was reborn in every Math class I ever took.

"But here, in your culture, it has the exact opposite meaning. Here, it means having the chance to do it again—to do it right, not the condemnation of having to do it again. I rather like yours."

As riveting as this high-minded philosophical discussion was, time was of the essence. Eventually, he continued. "So you will name me as the beneficiary of the insurance policy. That policy is for one million dollars."

"Right."

"The only stipulation—contingency, if you will—is I must give one-hundred thousand of the proceeds to this woman who is the mother to your child."

"Bingo."

"And how will we capture this agreement to everyone's

satisfaction?"

"Your word is good with me. I'll give you her name and address."

"You are a trusting soul."

"I don't have time not to be."

"And the deed to the diner?"

"That is going to the priest and my mother. Gonna use it as some kind of work-study thing or some shit."

"And you will start this wheel in motion, if you will, by…"

"When the date comes and I haven't paid what I owe someone will pay me a visit. This visit will put the wheels in motion. That's it."

"And you're fine with this?"

"Like you said, 'rebirth.' I'm going to start over."

"Don't worry. What you lose you regain—and then some—if you do it right."

"I'll let you know. I'll visit as a bird or some shit."

"Perhaps a fox."

* * *

A fox. I'm not entirely sure I possess the slyness required to be reborn a fox. The truth is — as one could see from the fucking mess I now found myself in — I am not as nearly as sly I thought I was.

I thought for a moment: Why, even with the prospect of my own violent demise looming, was I willing to even entertain the thought of — for all intents and purposes — removing myself from the face of the Earth for the benefit of bunch of twisted motherfuckers?

They were cocksuckers; the whole lot of them.

Della Pina never worked an honest day in his life. He may believe he lives by some sort of code, but there is no honor among thieves. I should know. That fucker has more blood on his hands than a bone saw operator at a slaughterhouse.

Tip is little more than a common street thug. His decision to hitch his wagon to Della Pina's star is proof he has little self-esteem. And the fact that I have given serious thought to faking my own death for the benefit of this meathead shows my own self worth is not much higher.

J? I've always enjoyed talking to the guy. But he's greedy. Out of all of us, he was the one cat living the American dream. But rather than be happy with the life he has built for himself here, he has fallen victim to the great American plague of wanting more, more, more.

The priest? Like so many members of the clergy, he's proven himself to be nothing more than a charlatan. He may be worse than all of these cocksuckers. And, he's fucking my mother. He's the devil with a collar. A dog with a collar.

But despite them all, there is my son. He is the lone reason I have given this idea any thought at all. I failed him in every way possible. I have not been present. I have not been a provider. I have not been a teacher. I have not been a father. As much as I want to be around him, I know that I will do him no good. But my disappearing from his life forever, I will finally be given the opportunity to provide for him. And that's an opportunity I cannot let pass.

CHAPTER NINE

Jesus Christ. I need this piece of work like I need a hole in my head. Wait, bad choice of words.

"So the policy you seek is for one million dollars of coverage."

"Yes. That's right."

"And the premiums would amount to…" He started punching in a bunch of numbers on the computer—his face about three inches away despite his coke-bottle glasses. This fucker couldn't get laid in a whorehouse or a morgue. If I thought he had ten-large on hand I'd have tied him up right then and there.

"Forty-six dollars and ten cents," he finished finally. "Paid monthly on the fifteenth of each month. Until you're seventy-two."

"Great. Totally doable." I couldn't help but laugh — forty-six dollars a month on a million-dollar policy for someone with my kind of lifestyle. Apparently someone paid a visit to this agent before I got here.

"You will need to pass a basic physical and fill out some

forms. I have a man in the next room who'll take your blood pressure and draw some blood."

"Great. We good?"

"We are good. It's such an odd transaction. You only make out if you aren't around to see it. Beats the grain mills though, the Cheerios smell notwithstanding."

"You'd be a big hit there for sure."

"The dust would not work with my asthma, I'm afraid."

I didn't even pretend to pay attention. I got up and headed for the little conference room. The only fly in the ointment was I am not a physical specimen. I'm not on death's door by any means — from natural causes anyway — but it could be an issue. I was never any good at tests.

I breathed deeply in through the nose and exhaled. I turned the knob and entered the room.

"This won't hurt a bit."

"Jesus fucking Christ."

Tip smiled broadly, sincerely. I should have known.

"Roll up your sleeve. Let's check your ticker."

"Should we even bother? Seems to me I'm passing this test no matter what kinda health I'm found to be in."

"Hey, you should be thanking me. That's a pretty low monthly premium I arranged. You're a smoker, after all," Tip said. "Anyway, bad health is better than no health. Either way, I get to make the call. So, I say we try it this way first. We spread the wealth this way, you know what I'm saying? Everybody wins."

"Well, I guess it's a matter of how you define winning."

"In your case? Living is winning."

I wasn't so sure, but I didn't bother arguing the point. Maybe, though, winning was dying. The more I began to think about it, getting whacked would bring closure. And closure, in a sense, is freedom. Would I be free in a new place, under a new name? Tip seemed to think so. But where is there freedom in not being able to ever return to what I've always known? Where is there freedom in not ever being able to see my son again? I didn't bother asking. It wasn't Tip's problem.

"You know where I'm headed yet?" I asked Tip.

"We ain't ready to cross that bridge."

"But do you know?"

"Maybe I do. Like I said though, now ain't the time."

"Didn't you once tell me, 'no better time than the present'?"

"Yeah. And I'm telling you now to shut the fuck up. I'm beginning to lose my patience with you, Tommy. Not another word."

"I'm worth more to you now alive than dead."

"Maybe that's true. But I put a bullet in your head

today, I don't end up in a soup line tomorrow. I'd be fine. You keep pushing my buttons, kid, and we'll find a hole for you. I wouldn't lose a wink of sleep. You wanna help your kid, you'll shut up now. If not, keep talking. I don't give a good goddamn what happens to that boy of yours. Like I told you before, he ain't my concern. You keep your mouth closed, and I'll see to it he's taken care of. Not because I care, but because that's the deal. I mean what I say, I say what I mean. This is business. But I have no problem smokin' you, Tommy. Won't be the first time I smoked someone. And it wouldn't be the first time I walked away from being paid, either."

Part of me wished for a bullet in my head. But the other part of me was focused on my son.

"Just be thankful this exam doesn't include a prostate check," Tip said laughing. "Especially the kind where you feel both hands on your shoulders."

Maybe not, yet some how, it still felt like I was taking it right up the ass.

* * *

So we know how the movie is going to end. Two in the hat, a newly wealthy Hindu, a kid with a shot to get out, and a guinea mobster with a debt he'll never collect. Fuck him. Serves him right. I never fucked with him— on purpose — so if I've got to go at least he gets nothing.

"Oh, fuck," I said, connecting the dots for the first time.

"What's up?" Tip asked, snapping to in the silence of the Caddy's air-tight cabin.

"You're going to shake down J for the $10k. That's why you were posing as the blood-taker at the insurance office."

"I thought drawing blood was nicely, ironic, didn't you?"

"Hilarious. Don't give up the night job."

I thought a bit longer. "Just don't kill him. He's a good guy and he's doing me a solid. He won't want to fight. Just show the gun and he'll fork the cash over."

***

We pulled into the entrance for Tift Farm. Very quickly, the view out the windshield went to jet-black as Tip cut the lights. More a park than a farm, Tift is where city people went to get some nature time. Its woods, big grassy fields, marshes and ponds were a little green oasis beside the expressway. Right under the Skyway that connected downtown and South Buffalo. For this reason, you were much more likely to find a burned out car or a severed thumb than Bambi. And the green, well, that had more to do with the toxins that polluted the grounds than it did with Mother Nature.

"Meeting time," Tip said getting out. "Time to plan our work and work our plan as they say."

"Maybe shake J down for $25 extra and see if you can

get the mayor to change it from Tift Farm to Tip Farm. Naming rights, ya know?"

"Such a clever mind gone to waste," he said fairly happily. "We'll see about that."

As we walked I could see the rear fender of my mother's 1988 gold Caprice Classic. There were people inside. I couldn't make them out in the impenetrable dark until Tip opened the back door and we got in.

"Forgive us, Father, for we have sinned. But I think we know what we're doing."

"Let's hope so, Tip. We've got seven days to make this work. Let's review the plan again."

"Salt water taffy?" Ma offered hopefully.

***

Tip and the priest shook hands.

"Father, how the hell are ya? Always a pleasure."

"I'm well, Tip. Thank you," the priest replied as he looked out the window into the blackness. "You know, it's ironic. They call this a nature preserve, but it's little more than a toxic waste dump. Things don't thrive here. They die here. This isn't exactly Love Canal, mind you, but I wouldn't drink the water here. I've always assumed that characterizing this place as a nature preserve was merely an extension of the dry, cynical humor that permeates this fine city. Either way, it's hard to escape pollution in Buffalo. Whether it's from the factories or the politics, like God, it's omnipresent. Maybe even more so."

"I suppose," Tip said. "You can polish a turd but it's still a turd."

"Something like that."

My mother turned around in her seat and held the box of taffy out toward Tip.

"No thanks, honey."

Mom shrugged and turned back around. "More for me, I guess."

"Let's get down to brass tacks," said the priest. "Obviously this plan hinges on Tommy's mythical demise. We all understand what we are gaining. But we need a little more light here. Namely, when Tommy goes underground, where exactly is he being reborn? His mother has the right to know, does she not?"

"Well, as you know, I'm handling Tommy's relocation. This isn't a fuckin game. His death will be faked. But let's get this straight: even though he's still gonna be alive, it will seem like he's dead. Mom, I'm sorry, but you ain't being told shit. As you know, Father, you can't be resurrected until you die. Once Tommy is reborn, his old life and all his ties to it will be over. It can't work any other way. There'll be no more Tommy. That guy's gone forever. If he turns up – or even a trace of him—and it comes out I didn't do my job, I'm gone. Dead. That can't happen. "

My mother turned around suddenly and hurled the box of taffy, striking Tip between the eyes. "How dare you tell me I have no right to know the whereabouts of my son. I carried him inside me for nine months. And despite the hell he's put me through he's still my son and he always will be, you motherless cunt." (So, she wasn't ready to abandon me, after all.)

Tip laughed in a controlled and somewhat menacing way, pushing the box of taffy that was now resting on his lap down onto the floorboard. "I understand," he said. "And despite your words, I do got a mother of my own and she'd feel the same as you. But this is business. It's life and death. Like I told you all, this ain't a fuckin game. There ain't any room for emotion here. We can't let the heart get in the way of the brain. If that happens, we're fucked. And if we fuck this up, Tommy dies for real. And so will others—some of whom are in this very vehicle."

"I'll be alright, ma," I said, not necessarily knowing if that were true. "I'm gonna be fine."

"We're all gonna be alright," said Tip, trying to bring the temperature down. "Just let me handle everything."

"My only concern," I said, knowingly talking out of turn and doing so somewhat nervously, "is how you are going to handle J. He's a good man. I don't want anything happening to him." Expressing that concern to Tip on our way here was one thing. That was between us. But now it was out there in front of the others. I knew I had crossed a line. Tip shot me a look, and if looks could kill, I'd be a dead man.

"Just what are your intentions, Tip?" Father Frank asked. "I think we have the right to know the particulars of this plan."

"Like I said, padre: Just let me handle things."

"Think about it, Father. He's setting J up. He has to be. It makes perfect sense. In fact, it's the only thing that makes sense."

Even as I spoke these words, I could not believe they were coming out of my mouth. I believed them to be true, of course, but by spewing them in front of other parties I was, at the very least, putting myself — and, at most, putting everyone else — in immediate jeopardy.

"You fucking son-of-a-bitch!" Tip barked as he lunged across the backseat. He grabbed me by the collar and slammed my head into the side window. "I've had enough of you and your fucking mouth. I swear to God I will pop you right here. I will fucking end your life, you worthless cock-sucking mick!"

"Get your grease-ball hands off of my son, you guinea cocksucker," my mother screamed.

Tip turned quickly around and backhanded my old lady,

sending her crashing into the passenger window. I caught Tip with a left to the face, but it was completely without effect. Tip then turned toward me and drove his large, meaty fist squarely into the side of my head. It was like being hit at pointblank range with a cannon ball and I felt my brain slam into the right side of my skull. Before I even had the chance to recover, Tip delivered another crushing blow to my head. It was like being hit with a wrecking ball.

"You dumb, motherfucking piece of white-trash shit, I'll kill…"

And then it all happened so fast.

I felt the warm splatter of blood spray across my face before I even heard the blast. It felt like a dream. I opened my eyes and there was Father Frank, turned squarely around in the driver's seat, still holding the gun. I then looked to my side and there was Tip, a bloody and lifeless mess with a hole in his head the size of a baseball.

Shit was real now and we were in up to our knees.

* * *

"Anything you'd like to confess, Father?"

The scene had now gone officially absurd. Up until this point, it had all felt a bit like a movie. I was looking at myself and the whole thing from the outside —detached. Maybe I was dreaming. Superman would fly out of the phone booth and the alarm would go off just in time to start another gray day.

I pinched myself. No dream.

And now, there was this, a giant grotesque sucking sound coming from Tip's head.

"How deep do you suppose the pond is?" my mother asked. My fucking mother, for Christ sakes!

"Eighteen, twenty maybe," Padre said.

"What are you two, Bonnie and Clyde?"

"Tommy, get up front. You drive."

"Wait," the priest said. "We roll it into the pond, I get that. But is there something we can do to throw them off the scent a little bit when they do find him?"

"A calling card?" I asked.

"Right," he said.

"Little John Coniglio always slashes the throat. The hole in the head takes that off the table."

"But it's my car," said my mother. "It's going to come back to me either way."

"What if it was stolen?" Padre asked.

"What if it was stolen? Yeah, stolen after a home invasion. What if Tip and Carlo kicked the door in looking for me? You told them to fuck off and eventually they left?"

"And I tell the cops that Tip— who I'll just call the other guy —seemed uncomfortable with the whole thing. He tells

Carlo, 'Come on. She's an old lady. She doesn't know anything.'
They argue for a while and then leave."

"Then they find the car and Tip."

"What's my alibi? Where am I?"

"Confession," he said. "I'm a priest. I can't divulge
what's said in a confessional. Then, we went for a cup of coffee."

"And I know just the place," I nodded. "You own it."

* * *

Father Frank and I jumped out of the car and walked to
the back.

"Open the trunk," the priest said.

"Why?" the old lady protested.

"Just open the fucking trunk," Father Frank demanded in
an uncharacteristically profane manner. "I need the damn toolbox."

"This isn't the time for engine work," I cracked.

"Funny," said the priest. "It's not auto repair that I have
in mind. We're gonna do a little dental work."

"What the fuck?"

"You want them running dental records on this guy when
they find him?"

"Good point."

I reached into the car and pushed Tip's body down
across the seat. The priest opened the back passenger-side door,

sat down and placed Tip's head on his lap. He then pulled open the gangster's mouth and reached in with pliers. It was the Little Shop of Horrors, live in my mother's back seat.

"Almost done," said the priest, shoving each extracted tooth into his inside coat pocket with his blood-soaked fingers.

"Wait a minute!" my mother exclaimed. "Fingerprints. This piece of shit has gotta have a record. They can run his fingerprints to identify him!"

"It's a good thing you watch all those cop shows," I said.

"Don't be a wise ass."

The priest got out of the car, reached back in and pulled Tip's body down so that it was now lying across the floorboard.

"Get his feet," he said to me. "Help me turn him over so that he's laying on his stomach."

I did as the priest said. Father Frank grabbed Tip's hands and pulled them toward him so that his arms and hands were hanging outside the car. The priest then put Tip's hands on the ground.

"Hand me that pick axe from the bottom of the toolbox."

The scene was now beyond sick and officially had reached cartoonish. I handed the axe to Father Frank and turned my head away. Thwack, thwack. Tip's fingers were now in the priest's jacket along with his teeth.

"Nice job," my mother said, reaching for another piece

of saltwater taffy. "We'll build a fire when we get home tonight and cremate everything. Teeth burn, right?"

Who the fuck were these two people I was with? Were I not now faced with spending the rest of my life in Attica, I would have laughed.

"C'mon," Father Frank said. "Let's roll the car down."

We stuffed Tip back into the car, and then the priest and I walked to the rear. The priest put the toolbox back in the trunk and then told my mother to get ready. She pushed the throttle to neutral and stood outside, her left hand on the side of the windshield and right hand on top of the steering wheel.

"On the count of three," the priest said. "One… two… three… push!"

The old lady's Caprice was a tank, but once we got it rolling its own weight carried it quickly toward the water.

"Outta the way, ma," I yelled. She let go of the wheel and quickly moved away from the car, watching as the priest and I ran by, pushing the vehicle toward the dark waters. Without signaling one-another, we stopped simultaneously and watched as the Caprice slowly sank, lowering Tip to his watery grave. Father Frank blessed himself and asked for forgiveness. I blessed myself and prayed that I not get jammed. The thug's blood was now dried on my face, cemented there by the cool and constant Western New York breeze of late October. Nothing good ever happens in October, I thought. It is the cruelest of months.

"Take a bath, you no-good guinea wop," my mother said. She hiked up her dress, squatted and began to pee. "It's not on his grave, but close enough."

"Frances! Enough! Do you realize what we've done?" the priest asked.

"He got what he deserved," said the old lady.

I walked down to the water's edge and splashed my face over and again, then raised the end of my shirt to wipe it dry.

"You'll need to burn that shirt," Father Frank said.

"I'll put it in the fire along with Tip's fingers and teeth. Shit, we just need to burn everything."

"I pray that excludes our eternal souls."

"Let me ask you, Padre, can angels swim?"

"We've no time for riddles."

"Find time. I think we just rolled my Guardian Angel into the drink."

"Guardian Angel? I think you've been in the drink. He was no angel on your shoulder. Those were his boots. They were forcing you under the water. Now you're a nose above. Time to decide if we're going to sink or swim."

"Maybe this fucking cesspool is holy water."

"We're not clean yet, but we're getting there."

Chapter Ten

"The thing about coffee," J said earnestly, " is that when it's too hot it becomes bitter. Not hot enough and it just doesn't taste right."

"Like the bears and the porridge," I said.

J's blank expression said everything.

"Now, the flattop is an amazing invention. It heals itself, maintains itself, so long as you do a few simple things to take care of it," he said, scraping remnants of egg, hash, home fries and who knows what into its gutter with a flat piece of metal about the size of a cleaver but without any handle. "Just scrape it regularly, keep it hot, and clean out the gutter and it will be fine. The oil and grease protect it. It actually gets better with use. More flavor is conveyed from it to that which it's cooking."

"That's fucking deep for eggs," I said out of genuine appreciation.

"'Tis hatched and shall be so.' Shakespeare." A fucking Indian quoting Shakespeare: Shit, indeed, was getting weird.

J held my gaze intently. Really piercingly. "Now, the

alarm is over here. When your mom or the priest leaves, tell em'
to set it. I will leave the code blank for you to program yourself.
When they come in, punch in the code. My suggestion is to give
it to no one. If it goes off, the police are automatically notified.
They will receive a call too. We must call the company to switch
the number from mine to theirs."

"Got it. Ever need it?"

"Yes. A few times. Usually false alarms. A drunk not
realizing it's the middle of the night. Things like that. But once
there was a break in."

"Get anything?"

"I never keep cash in the register over night. I suggest
you do the same."

"Trust me. Cash stays with me."

"Any other questions?"

"What are you going to do with yourself now that you're
not slinging hash?"

"I would like to see the American West. The Grand Can-
yon. Hollywood. And that place where they have all those nice
automobiles stuck halfway in the ground."

"Cadillac Ranch?"

"Yes, Cadillac Ranch. Why all those cars in the ground?
Very American."

"Sounds cool, " I said. "Good luck with that."

"And good luck to you—whatever that might mean in this situation."

"You have the ten grand on you? Here is the insurance certificate," I said reaching into my coat.

J looked at it front and back.

"You will pay me $100 per week for 100 weeks—essentially two years. That's the repayment schedule."

"No interest?"

"No. They will assume the mortgage, which is quite reasonable, upkeep, maintenance and taxes. I am signing everything over to them. They may also change the name if they wish."

"No way. JJ's is an institution. The name stays."

"As you wish. And now for the ten thousand," he said pulling out his phone. "I will have it brought here."

I put my hand on his. "It's all good."

* * *

The priest rolled in five minutes after I left.

"The story has changed some. But the ending is still the same. That's the important part."

"So I have heard," J said. "You could wait no longer?"

"He forced my hand. I think it's still clean. Your brother has been avenged. The guilty have paid."

"And now the innocent shall be set free."

* * *

Terms had been reached with J, Tip wasn't in the picture anymore, I was going to have ten grand to get me started and the priest and mom were getting the deed to the diner. There was only one last visit to pay, and that was to my kid who was about to profit from my disappearing act. Though he was too young to realize he was at a fork in the road. Either cash in off my departure, or suffer the hardship of my hanging around.

When I arrived at Katie's, she let me in without hesitation. It was a rare move. Normally, she stands her ground in the doorway and keeps me outside. Not this time. Whether it was a bittersweet moment for her, I can't say. But I do know she recognized that this was the last time she would see me and that it would be my last time seeing our son.

"Youur friend came to see me the other night," said Katie.

"Yeah, well, he won't be coming around any more. That I can guarantee."

"Should I ask?"

"No you shouldn't. The less you know the better. You're protected that way. Besides, it'll give you nightmares."

"You know what you're doing, Tommy?"

"Sure I do."

"No, I don't mean are you aware of what you are doing. I mean, do you have this figured out?"

"You know me, Katie. I never have nothing figured out, even when I say that I do you know damn well that I don't. This, where I'm ending up, was never supposed to be left up to me in the first place. It was all being arranged. But, things have changed a bit. So, now, though, I guess it's up to me to figure out myself. And that's something I ain't done yet."

Katie stared into my eyes and shook her head.

"You always been a fucking idiot," she said. Then she smiled, slightly.

"That's the nicest thing you said to me in a while."

"So where is he?"

"He's upstairs. It's late. He's sleeping."

"Can I… "

"Of course. Try not to wake him. You wake him up and I kill you myself."

I walked up the stairs slowly. Halfway up, the wood creaked. I cringed, worrying the sound would wake Thomas. I looked back down at Katie who was sitting on the couch watching me. She waved me on. "Go. Go, he's fine. That happens all the time."

Upon reaching the top of the stairs, I entered his room and found him in his tiny Mickey Mouse toddler bed, lying there in the glow of the nightlight plugged into the wall next to where he slept. He had kicked the covers off and was laying at a right angle. He was beautiful.

I reached down and straightened him out so that his head was resting square on his pillow. Then I pulled the small blue comforter up to his chin. I brushed his blond hair across his forehead and his eyes opened half way. He reached up with both arms as if he wanted me to pick him up. I smiled and his tiny hands lightly touched my face. But the Sandman had too tight a hold on him, and before he could open his eyes fully, he was fast asleep again.

I could feel my eyes begin to well up with tears. His entire life flashed before me: His first day of school, his baseball games, his prom, graduation, college and wedding. I would miss them all. I believed he would be OK. I believed he would be happy. I bent down and kissed him on the cheek and then gently stroked his cheeks with the back of my hand and watched him dream. And I wondered whether years from now if he would ever dream of me.

* * *

I waited a moment so that I could regain my composure before returning downstairs and taking a seat on the couch next to Katie.

"Listen, as you know, arrangements have been made so that Thomas is taken care of. Be smart. Put that money some-where. You'll need to make sure it's hidden, at least for a while.

Hide it from everyone because there ain't a fucking person we know whom you can trust. And you can't just go and run to the bank with it and make a deposit. You can't do anything that's going to send a red flag. And don't go buying new shit, either. Don't do anything that will call attention to yourself. Just let it sit there."

"You think I'm an idiot? Jesus, Tommy, gimme some credit. Besides, all those years I spent with you, you don't think I learned a thing or two about hiding shit?"

"I just don't want anything happening. I wanna make sure he's set. And I don't want you getting in any trouble. I ain't ever been in a position to really take care of my kid. If I can pull this off, at least I will have done something good. It ain't been often in my life when I'm able to say that."

"And whose fault is that?"

"You don't think I know that?"

"What could have been, Tommy... Fucking idiot."

"You still wonder?"

"I don't now. I did then. You never could do nothing the right way; or the smart way. I stuck around for as long as I could take it. But there comes a time when you have to say 'enough's enough.' I probably shoulda said that long before I did, but I said it eventually. You left me no other choice. So, do I wonder? I did wonder. Not no more."

"Well, I'm paying for that now."

"Maybe a little too much."

"Maybe so."

"I used to think you deserved what was coming to you. But I dunno if anyone deserves something like this. Maybe you got one too many chances. Maybe had you got jammed up for a while, you would have learned your lesson and it wouldn't have come to this. I dunno, Tommy. Nothing with you was ever easy. Maybe this was inevitable."

"Just promise me one thing, Katie. Promise me he doesn't turn out like me."

"I don't need to make that promise to you, Tommy. I made that promise to myself the second that boy came outta me. He may look like his daddy, but I'll be damned if he's gonna be like him."

I couldn't help but chuckle.

"I might not have deserved you, but he sure as hell does."

"Damn fucking straight," Katie said. And then she smiled.

"You gonna be alright Tommy?"

"You know how every time you've ever asked me that, I always told you 'yes.' This time, though? Well, I really don't fucking know."

CHAPTER ELEVEN

"Jealous of all these kids with their foot-long crosses? Need a little more bling, Father?"

"I'm a gangsta for God. On the inside."

"As it should be. What can I help you with, Father?"

"A wedding ring. Two wedding rings, actually."

Hanlon looked at him over his bifocals. "Something you want to tell me, Father?"

"Not for me. Not for me. They're gifts. A couple kids about to learn the meaning of the word 'commitment.'"

"Got it. I wish more of these fucking savages, forgive me, would do the same. Running round wild as Indians. I think it's because they don't have no place to go—no one to go home to."

"I think that's truer than you know."

"I'd be out there myself if I was twenty-something, no job, nobody nagging after me. In fact, a few nights ago I was down at Durkin's tipping a few and forgot my hat in here. I come in and fell asleep. Then I hear a commotion in the back.

Some fucker climbed in the window. I was so fucking blind on the juice I walked right past him and he got away. I put a shot past his ass but wasn't really trying. Just sending a message. He didn't make off with anything, but I wanted to let him know what would be waiting for him should he return."

"I have a feeling it was received. At least I hope so."

"That's as close as that prick is going to get to meeting his maker without actually touching his beard."

"Sometimes," the priest said, "it's a close shave these kids need most."

* * *

I said my goodbye to my boy and I made peace to the extent that I could with Katie. I had one more person on my list with whom I needed to have last words.

"I gotta say, ma, I thought for a long time I that I owed you an apology for being such a piece-of-shit son. But look at you now. What the hell has happened?"

"You got some nerve, Tommy. You put me through some real shit over the years; shit no mother should have ever had to go through. You've been a real bastard."

"I know, mom. I was a horrible son. I let you down — over and over. I know."

"Yes you did mister. You were an embarrassment. I deserved better, especially after your brother died. You should have been a better son. I needed you and you were never there. Instead, you were either in jail or on the street. And then when your father died, I had nobody. Jamie was always there for me. He was the kinda son that you shoulda been. But you ain't ever given a shit about anyone but yourself."

"Mom, I know… I just said I know I was a fuck up. But let's not make Jamie a saint. He killed himself. You wanna talk about selfishness? There ain't a more selfish act than that."

"Shut up! Just shut your fucking mouth! Jamie had problems. He was sick. He had the troubles. But he never brought shame on his family the way you did. My son, the criminal. You are a disgrace. When did you ever give me reason to be proud? You let me down. You let your father down. You let Katie down. And you let your son down. Shame on you."

"Well, whether you wanna believe it or not, ma, I always felt bad for being such a fuck up. But you know what? I don't so much anymore. Look at yourself, for Christ sake. You are sleeping with a goddamn priest, and a crooked priest at that."

"He has always been there for me, goddamn it. Unlike you. You think I'm proud of what's happened? And now — now, look at the shit we're in, all because of you."

"No, mom. You brought this shit upon yourself by running around with this fucking character. Then you two fucking nitwits concocted this whole thing like it's some fucking episode of 'Murder She Wrote.' But shit is about to get real. It's like you opened the fucking seventh seal or something."

Stopping was out of the question now even though I knew doing so was right. But shit, the genie was way, way out of the bottle.

"I'll say one thing: I ain't ever been nothing but a crook, but I never passed myself off any other way. That's more than anyone can ever say for Father Frank. Priest my ass. He's a fucking criminal just like me. I always owned it though. He's a fucking charlatan."

Silence fell over the room. My mother grabbed her pack of Winston's lying on the coffee table, pulled a cigarette out with her thumb and forefinger and tapped the butt on the table. Her hands were shaking.

" I dunno," she muttered quietly. "I dunno know what the hell I'm doing anymore."

I felt ashamed of myself; ashamed for what I put my mother through her whole life and ashamed for the way I treated her just now. I meant what I said, but I didn't need to say it. There was no need. In an argument like this, there is no winner. And the truth was, we were both fucking losers — me by fault and her by circumstance.

"Look, ma, what's done is done. Ain't nothing going to change what I did, or what you've done. What does matter though is that you're OK when I'm gone. I need to know he's going to take care of you. How I feel about him doesn't matter. What matters is how you survive all this."

She sat there on the couch, saying nothing and staring out the window.

"Ma? You gonna be OK?"

She turned her head toward me and exhaled, letting go a tight stream of cigarette smoke.

"I dunno," she said, tears filling up her eyes. "I don't fucking know anything anymore."

We sat there for a moment, saying nothing and then the front door opened. It was the priest.

"Thomas, I was just thinking of you," he said before turning his head toward my mother. The priest looked back at me with concern and then back again toward mom. "My dear, what's wrong?"

"What's wrong?" I barked. "Everything's wrong. Her son is about to fake his own death and she's involved in a murder. Really, you aren't that clueless, are you? All these years as a priest. Didn't any of God's all-knowing bullshit rub off on you?"

"It wasn't murder," the priest said firmly. "It was self–defense. *Your* defense." He looked back down at my mother. "Cast your burden upon the Lord and he will sustain you."

"Oh brother, spare us the godly bullshit, will you Frank?

You're associated with the mob, you fucking killed someone and you're fucking my mother! Shit, I'm more holy than you are at this point! Just fucking shut the fuck up!"

The priest looked stunned.

"Look, just take care of her, OK? That's all. Just make sure she is alright. You owe me that much for fuck's sake."

I got up and started heading for the door. Then, before exiting, I turned around and said: "And if they ever do come down on you two, take the fucking fall. Can you do that for her? Tell me you can do at least that, Frank. Think of it as your god-damn penance."

CHAPTER TWELVE

My head hurt. In fact, I cannot remember wanting a drink so fucking badly in my life.

Murphy's was happy to oblige. I ordered a beer and a shot, plus quarters for the jukebox — which stopped adding tracks around AC/DC's "Back in Black" album. While that may have been a good choice ("What Do You Do for Money, Honey?) I felt like something a bit more downbeat to fit the tone. So, I fed the machine a dollar, selected The Replacements and wallowed in Paul Westerberg's despair.

"Jaysus fucking Christ," the buxom bartender whom I'd never met before hissed. "Are you planning on suicide?"

"Sort of."

She poured herself a shot and then pushed one to me. "We're both going to need this at this rate."

I pulled out three crisp twenties.

"It's on me," she said. "You look like you could use one."

"I want to clear up my tab. It's under 'Patton'."

"Like the General? My father loved him."

"That's me. All blood and guts. Or will be," I added

under my breath.

"Got it. Says you're good."

"That's one word that's never been associated with me."

"Paid off today."

"By who?"

"Didn't happen while I was here. No idea. Why don't you take one of those quarters and play a happy song?'

The fucking irony. I've probably got hours to live, or live in this present incarnation anyway, and now pennies from heaven. I headed for the jukebox as directed and played CCR's 'Fortunate Son.'

"Much better," she said.

There was another shot on the bar in front of me.

"Are you hitting on me?"

"You wish," she purred. "It's from him," she said, tossing her head toward a booth in the corner.

* * *

J got up and walked over to where I was sitting.

"I didn't think your people hung out in places like this."

"It is a common misconception that my religion forbids alcohol," said J. "But I've come to expect ignorance as the rule."

"Well, most everyone thinks that my people do nothing but drink alcohol, and I'd say that perception is dead-on accurate."

"Yes, I suppose."

"People's ignorance notwithstanding J, you're not exactly a barfly."

"I suppose that's correct, as well."

"Thanks by the way for paying my tab. And thanks, too, for the drink."

"The least I could do."

"Anyway, back to the matter at hand. What brings you to Murphy's?"

"I thought I would find a place to have a drink and do some thinking. Many things are in my head right now."

"Care to share?"

"Just some business," J said. "I just have some business that I need to take care of and my thoughts must be clear."

"Business? You got some new venture now that you're no longer slinging hash?"

"Not new business. More like tying up loose ends on some old business that remains outstanding."

"Seems to me that's all that life is about: tying up loose ends."

"Yes, well, that may be. This is family business. That is business impossible to ignore."

"Oh Christ, family business. The messiest kinda business there is."

"There is no business more important," said J before changing the subject. "So, what is your plan?"

"I've said my goodbyes. I'm not long for this town. After I slip outta here, my mother reports me missing, the priest becomes the family spokesman, my criminal history and troubles with the mob fuel the mystery around my disappearance and moves the story along and it all goes from there."

"Are you at peace?"

"Of course not. I'm leaving my son. I've failed that kid since the day he was born and that will forever be my legacy to him."

"As I have assured you, he and his mother will be taken care of."

I didn't know what to say, so I said nothing. I finished my drink, and J finished his.

"You do for family whatever it is you must do," he said. "Good luck to you, my friend. I must go. As I said: I have some loose ends to tie up. Family business. Important business."

And with that, he was gone.

* * *

I stayed put in the booth and twirled the ice in J's otherwise empty glass. Family: Can't live with 'em, can't live without 'em,' as they say.

Wait... if I'm losing mine effectively by going on the

lamb, then why not just go out in a blaze of glory like Butch and Sundance in Bolivia? Buffalo is often thought of as the Bolivia of the Great Lakes…

I was getting crunchy.

I started to slide out of the booth to go to the bar and make a new tab when the jukebox got turned up. "Here Comes the Bride" in bagpipes.

I stopped. What the fuck? I know every goddamn track in the box and that ain't one of them. I sort of froze in place. I heard the little bell above the door jingle as the door opened.

Fuck me. This was some weird homage to Tarantino. I was getting smoked.

I turned around and there she was—all in white. Well, off-white, who we kidding? The priest was there in collar to her left. My mother was to her right. Her mother and my son were just behind.

I got that fluttering feeling in my eyelids and I felt my eyes kind of roll up toward the tin ceiling. I had an overwhelming hot flash, saw spots and that was that.

CHAPTER THIRTEEN

*H*e walked in through the back door.

The first guy was in the kitchen, standing in front of a stove, staring down into a pot of boiling water as he stirred what presumably was spaghetti or some other type of Dago food. As he approached, he picked up a pan from a metal table nearby and slammed it down to make his presence known. Spaghetti man looked up from his pot. Horrified, the color drained quickly from his face. A single bullet to the Adam's apple.

As he lowered the pistol, the gunman couldn't help but smile. There was something about the quiet sound of the silencer. He couldn't put his finger on it exactly, but it always made things a little more emphatic, he thought.

With the gun at his side, he moved through the kitchen into the hall that led into the bar and dining area. The second poor bastard never saw it coming as he emerged from the men's room. Talk about bad timing. He stared at the gunman who was making his way down the hall. Right between the eyes. He dropped like a sack of potatoes.

The dull thud startled the man in the dining room sitting with Carlo. He rose from his chair and reached into his blazer *for his piece. But before he could even pull his arm back out of his jacket, there were two bullets in his chest.*

Carlo sat at the table, staring up into the gunman's eyes. He tried to appear cool, but it would have been a safe bet the wiseguy's shorts were heavier than they were just minutes ago.

"Did you order the Chicken Tikkamissala?"

Carlo's eyes darted all around the room for help and henchmen.

"They're all gone, Carlo. All your fucking henchmen — gone, just like my brother."

Carlo raised his napkin to his face and wiped his mouth, then took a drink from his glass of wine.

"And so it goes..." he said, shrugging his shoulders.

"You know," Carlo continued, "I don't think we ever had your kind inside my club before."

"Well, you shouldn't keep the back door open. You know my kind of people cannot be trusted," J said, now sitting across from Carlo and pointing his gun at the mobster's chest.

"At one time, this was a nice little city. Good families. Good jobs. Guys working for the railroad and Bethlehem Steel. The OLV Basilica, it was the centerpiece of this community. You know, it's a national shrine, right? I married my wife there in 1958. Been with her since I was 17. Wonderful woman. I don't

know... Maybe I should have moved her the fuck outta here. Once the steel plant went, this place... well... And then, your people started moving in, all these fucking towel heads and shit. I don't have anything against them. But you know, when you come here, you play by the rules and if you don't, well, you suffer the consequences."

"Like my brother?"

"He owed me a substantial amount of money."

"So then why didn't you come and see me?"

"Look, I tried to work with him. He knew what would happen to him if he didn't pay. He begged that we not come to you. He didn't want you brought into this. He was worried about your business. We made a deal. Since he couldn't pay, I had him carry out a job for me. He did what we asked. But I can't have an outsider involved in my business, knowing things and shit like that. Surely, you understand. And so, he had to go. It was business. Just business."

J pushed himself out of his chair, the gun still pointing at Carlo, but now at his head.

"You're a fucking animal," J snarled, the gun in his hand shaking.

Carlo took another drink of wine but kept his eyes fixed on J. As he put his glass back down on the table, J cocked back his arm and swung roundhouse, pistol-whipping Carlo across the face with such force he was knocked off his chair and onto the floor on his stomach. J crouched down and stuck his knee into the small of Carlo's back and grabbed the mobster by the chin, pulling it up as if he were trying to pull the lid off a container.

"Just business, you say. Just business. Well, that's why I am here today. I have some business to take care of myself."

J smashed Carlo's bloody face into the floor. "Put your fucking hands behind your back."

Carlo did as he was told. J pulled out a plastic strip, wrapped it around Carlo's wrists and pulled it tightly through the fastener.

"Get the fuck up," said J.

He led Carlo through the social hall, taking him on a short tour of his dead soldiers before exiting through the back door. J reached into his coat and pulled out his car keys. As they reached his sedan, he opened the trunk and pointed inside with the end of his handgun.

"Get the fuck in the trunk," he told Carlo. "Get in the fucking trunk or I'll blow your fucking head off right here."

* * *

"I now pronounce you husband and wife." The priest turned to the bartender, my mother, Katie's mother, our son and the picture of OJ that hung above the register.

"Ladies and Gentlemen, please join me in celebrating

the holy matrimony of," he looked down at a 3x5 index card in his bible, "John Francis McGuire and Mary Catherine Cunningham."

The applause was sparse but sincere. This wasn't how I envisioned getting married. It surely wasn't how she envisioned getting married. But it happened. I think.

"You may now kiss the bride."

I did.

We sat together at a booth while the bartender poured shots of Crown Royal and drew tall pints for all.

"Is this real? Did that really happen?"

"It did. It's real. You can't run any more."

"Ironically, that's what the rest of our lives will be. Running."

"Not necessarily. Your mom's boyfriend is a clever one."

"I smell our first married argument."

"He came to see me and spelled the whole thing out. I thought he was fucking nuts and told him so. But when I thought about it...it made sense. You're a fucking idiot but I've loved you since we were kids. And now we have a kid. That kid needs a father like I need a husband."

I'm not a crier, but my eyes welled up. Even if someone blew into the bar right now and put two in my hat, I'd heard what I needed to hear. Everything else is gravy.

"Well, I guess then you're in luck. How do you feel about Florida? I'm sick of this fucking snow."

"My mom got you a shovel for a wedding present. You ain't going anywhere."

* * *

J drove down Ridge Road toward Route 5 along the lake, the muffled sounds of Carlo coming through the backseat from the trunk where the mob boss had been stuffed with his hands tied behind his back and a rag shoved into his mouth. As he headed south, J wondered to himself whether he was having an out-of-body experience. Physically, he was behind the wheel manning the automobile down the highway. Yet, mentally, he actually could see himself floating along the outside of the vehicle, looking in and witnessing the events unfold as if he were watching a movie starring himself.

One after another, J passed the once bustling and now abandoned buildings of Bethlehem Steel that dotted the sides of the highway like a rash. The enormous plant that once pumped life into Lackawanna now lay dormant and rotting like a corpse — a constant, haunting reminder not only of the city's thriving past but also its current lifelessness. Continuing down the highway, J passed a series of blue-collar bars, gas stations and the landmark Dickie's donut shop as he headed in the direction toward the Ford stamping plant. He then turned right off Route

5 toward the entrance of Woodlawn Beach, a one-mile stretch of sand along the lake that in the 1970s was a well-known homosexual gathering place the locals not so affectionately referred to as Gay Bay.

J drove to the end of the dead-end road, turning his lights out so he would not draw any attention despite the fact it was now close to 2 a.m. and late October, when the area's beaches were essentially barren. Upon parking, he walked to the back of the car, opened the trunk and pulled Carlo out on to the ground, pushing him toward the dunes, which they then proceeded to trudge over on their way down to the water.

"Hold it right here," said J, pulling back on Carlo's hand restraint as if it were a horse's rein.

"I am going to afford you a luxury that you denied my brother," he said to Carlo. "You gave him the impression he would live if he did what you asked of him. Instead, you put two bullets in the back of his head. The back of his head, which means he did not see it coming. You are a fucking coward. You do not deserve it, but I will not deny you the opportunity to look into my eyes. It is only right."

Carlo mumbled through the rag in his mouth. Exactly what he said could not be determined, but it was not exactly a "thank you." Carlo grunted again, this time, much louder. J walked toward him, put his left hand on Carlo's shoulder, pulled the mobster toward him and plunged a butcher's knife into his stomach. Carlo let out a muffled groan and fell back. J watched Carlo stagger for a second and then pushed him down into the sand. He unbuttoned Carlo's pants and pushed them down about six inches. Then, he grabbed the mob boss's member and with a single upward swipe, sliced it clean off. Carlo tried to let out a cry but instead began choking on the rag. J pulled the cloth from the gangster's mouth, replacing it with the old man's dick. Carlo, gagging on his own severed penis, stared up at J in horror.

J reached into his jacket and pulled out his pistol. The silencer was still attached. J pointed the gun at Carlo's head. This time, his hand was steady. All it took was a single shot, placed perfectly between the old man's eyes.

J stood there for a moment as the water touched the shore and then receded. A puddle of crimson began to spread in the sand under Carlo, his lifeless eyes wide open and his appendage still in his mouth. From his pocket, J pulled out a card and scribbled a note, which he placed just under Carlo's chin. "Tastes like chicken," it said.

CHAPTER FOURTEEN

"**M**ore to the right. It's not straight," she said with exasperation. "It's got to be on the level."

"How's this?"

"Better, but not great. Screw it in. Close enough."

The sign was new. The name was not.

Well, not entirely.

* * *

"These eggs are pretty good. Not bad at all," the lieutenant said. "Where'd you learn to cook like that? Seminary?"

"Army," the ex-priest said. "Stomachs and souls. We ministered to both."

"That where you got the idea for this? 'JJ's Holy Hash.' Kinda catchy."

"Sometimes things just come together. It's all part of the Lord's plan."

"Was schtupping the widow there part of the plan too, padre?"

He didn't even look up—just kept flipping the potatoes on the flattop. "God only knows," he said with a grin the cop couldn't see but could probably feel.

"And he aint tellin."

"More coffee?" he said with a big smile. This time he held the cop's gaze firm with his own. There was a long, pregnant pause.

"So a piece of shit gangster goes missing. Nobody knows nothing. Except that he was looking for your prodigal son."

"He was with me."

"Where was that again?"

"Church. The confessional." He poured the coffee.

"And with that collar you're not at liberty to say what you may have talked about. Am I right?"

He leaned very close to the cop. He was grinning, smirking really, and his eyebrows were arched to sharp points.

"Looks like the only collar here is mine."

The cop smiled now too. "You know what? I have a confession to make too." Now he leaned forward until they were nose to nose. "I don't give a fuck. I don't care where he is and I ain't looking. Maybe he took a vacation."

"Maybe the beach."

"Maybe the beach. What do I owe you Father?"

"Same as always from now on. Nothing. And you can call me Frank. I've turned in my resignation to the Archdiocese. I'm going civilian."

"Good luck, Frank. It's a jungle out there."

"Tell me."

CHAPTER FIFTEEN

And so here I am: living on funny money from a scam set up by a dead gangster whose teeth and fingers tips are keeping my mother's house warm, back together with the mother of my child thanks to the priest who's been banging my mom, and free from the harm of a ruthless crime boss whose head is now full of holes courtesy of a Middle Eastern egg scrambler living the American Dream.

Shit, it's been a fucking ugly game so far. I have no business at all still being in it, yet, I have the ball again and it's first down and ten. To my right, there's an angel. To my left, a devil. God's final test. One last drive. And there ain't a soul in this hard-luck town who's got their money on me to win.

As I lay awake, I find peace in the symphony of alternating breaths that come from my son and Katie, who sleep soundly next to me. One inhales, the other exhales; one exhales, the other inhales. The rhythm is as perfect as they are.

Slowly, I pull myself away, trying not to wake either of them. I put my feet on the floor, pull on my jeans, slip on my shoes, grab my coat off the chair next to the bed and sneak downstairs. I head to the kitchen, where I find the keys to Katie's car on the counter. Leaving the house, I am met by the crisp Buffalo air and as I get behind the wheel, I look up into the radiant morning sky.

I drive and drive and I give it no thought. My mind wanders, bouncing between thoughts of my father and grandfather, scooping grain day-in and day-out, year after year for decades upon decades. I travel without aim as I contemplate those at Mass who gather out of habit, out of obligation, out of tradition, praying out of fear, guilt and desperation. Further and further I drive unaware, as I think about Katie and Thomas and my mother and J. I think about the evil that sometimes comes from those who are sworn to do good and consider what lurks beneath the preserve and the spirit that haunts the dunes along the beach. I drive and I drive, along the water on Route 5, past the Ford plant and continue toward the lake, stopping, finally, where the gravel meets the sand.

I exit Katie's car, leaving the keys in the ignition and step onto the beach. I walk straight ahead, without thought yet with purpose, toward the water and into the water. It is cold and rough and I continue to forge ahead. The water is up to my knees, up to my thighs, up to my waist, up to my chest and I stop and look above. The clouds are moving, sunlight faintly breaking through. I turn around and lean backward, letting the water consume me. I am submerged, save for my mouth, nose and eyes.

I am cold.

I am sorry.

I am cleansed.

And I'd like to think that God gives us credit for trying.

— END —

EPILOGUE

Technically it was a neutral site, but Delaware Park was clearly much more of a home game for the North Side club than the South Buffalo team. Nothing in Buffalo is much more than twenty minutes by car from anywhere else, but the Frederick Law Olmsted park was closer to two minutes for the team that hailed from the once Italian but now mixed neighborhood south of Hertel and North of Jewett. It was mixed income and denomination. Mostly middle-class, these kids looked and acted like Anywhere USA — like a McDonald's commercial featuring 12-year olds playing soccer on a fall afternoon.

The park was uniquely, lovably, and quintessentially Buffalo. Doubtful Olmsted envisioned its wide green dotted with several baseball and softball diamonds with several outfields being very definitely 'in play' for the eighteen-hole Muni golf course that shared grass with them. Many the golfer pulled up short when a baseball rolled between his legs or even hit him hard on one hop. Similarly, sheepish golfers would quickly dart in between the drawn-in left fielder and the straightaway center-fielder, retrieving an errant shot.

It was a big beautiful mess.

The lone regulation-size soccer field was situated on the south side of the park, practically on top of the expressway that cut the park in two. Soccer had not caught on in Buffalo as it had in nearly every other American city. Interestingly, it had caught on massively in Buffalo's suburbs. But suburbs are, in the end, nearly all identical regardless of the metro they orbit.

Cities, though, were all different. Perhaps Buffalo was more different still.

The South Buffalo team looked like any team that could have come from there over the past hundred or more years. The Irish enclave was largely unchanged. There were still the Lace Curtain contingent with pictures of the Kennedys on the mantle and "Mary on the Halfshell" in their perfectly manicured back yards. There was a smaller contingent, largely in the Old First Ward, that was rougher. Same red or raven hair. Same pale skin. Loads of freckles. They were like a lot of banty roosters; not big, but not shy and usually tough as nails.

Their parents were slightly more bloated versions of the same.

Soccer may not have had the rabid following of hockey, football or baseball, but if your kid played it, every tilt was a cage match. South Buffalo parents did not get the memo that everybody gets a trophy or that it's all about participation, 'trying,' and building self-esteem.

Guaranteed, before every single South Buffalo kid got out of the car, either the mom or dad would turn to them in the back seat, look them hard in the eye, and say something to the tune of "no prisoners."

That was it. Message sent. Message received.

On this day, it was a good tussle. Nil-nil (in soccer parlance) until midway through the second half. The North side scored a beautiful goal by a Brazilian boy whose small stature belied his immense skill. He trapped a long pass, deked toward the corner, turned it inside and ripped the ball into the upper ninety (in soccer parlance) from thirty yards or better while the goalie literally stood stock still. This was not a shot they'd worked on in practice on Seneca Street.

From that point on, the North Side kids ran the equivalent of basketball's "four corners" offense. They passed front to back, side to side, in a game of keep away that was as effective as it was demoralizing for the South.

The Brazilian boy got the ball in the left corner and did a few lavish step-overs, taunting the fullback. This went on for a few tortuous seconds.

"Get the fucker!" a parent howled from the crowd.

The boy, perhaps in response, but likely not, put his cleats on top of the ball and waited for the defender to make his move and come to him.

He charged.

The Brazilian's eyes widened. A slight smile reached his lips. This would be his Sports Center moment. Just as the back closed in he'd spin, carry along the end line and cross or even shoot if the opportunity presented itself.

About five feet out, just as the Brazilian started his spin, the Southsider lowered his head, stretched out his arms and put his shoulder right into the smaller kid's breast bone. He wrapped, and drove him to the ground in a perfect form tackle. He rode over the top of the Brazilian boy's body as they hit the ground and kneed him hard in the ear as their progress finally was halted.

Whistles blew, players encircled them and parents streamed on the field. Police on horseback nearby galloped over and dispersed the adults. Coaches got players separated.

The South Buffalo kid was grabbed by the collar amidst the melee. His father was dragging him to the car. He didn't know if it was out of anger for what he'd done or simply for his protection. One glance up and he knew.

The father winked at him quickly. "We'd better hustle."

"Piece of shit, you fucking cocksucker!" an opponent's mom shouted, still on the field.

The Irish boy turned to face her, still pulled by the scruff of the collar by his father.

And then he shouted:

"Fuck yiz all!"

ACKNOWLEDGMENTS

Pat: Many thanks to my wife and children, parents and friends from the neighborhood. Special thanks to esteemed Buffalonian and professor, Dr. Matthew O'Brien, and editor par excellence Deena Kimmel, for their meaningful contributions.

Matt: Thanks to the City of Buffalo for being so inspiring and weird; to Patrick King and Sandra Block for the periodic and motivating lit talk; to NFB; to Deena Kimmel and Steve DeMeo for their work; to Amy for your tirelessness, Sophie for your support, Sam for your humor and Mimi for your fandom; and to anyone who reads this.

About the Authors

J. Matthew Smith grew up in Buffalo and now lives with his wife, Amy, and two children in Albany, N.Y. An award-winning journalist, he has worked for a number of daily newspapers and The Associated Press, and is also the author of "Jailed By My Father: Tales of Tough Love, Bad Haircuts and O.J." He wishes he played in the NHL.

Patrick Reynolds lives with his wife and two children outside Boston. He and his wife attended the same smallish parochial school in North Buffalo just one grade apart. They have no recollection of one another until twenty years later when they bumped into each other in Delaware Park. Different circles.